The Secret Sex Lives
of Wanda Mitty

FELIX BARON

T0317984

mischief

Mischief
An imprint of HarperCollins*Publishers*
77–85 Fulham Palace Road,
Hammersmith, London W6 8JB

www.mischiefbooks.com

A Paperback Original 2013

First published in Great Britain in ebook format by
HarperCollins*Publishers* 2012

A catalogue record for this book is
available from the British Library

ISBN-13: 9780007553365

Find out more about HarperCollins and the environment at
www.harpercollins.co.uk/green

CONTENTS

CONTENTS

Chapter One

Commuting by subway can be inspirational. When you drive, you get to see all sorts of interesting people, but just quick glimpses, in passing. On the subway you get to study them, sometimes up close, and your mind is free to wander. Yes, Wanda had been known to pass her stop a few times but that's better than rear-ending a bus because you're daydreaming. She knew that from bitter experience.

A businessman got up. Wanda slipped into his spot, next to a little sparrow of a woman whose skinny lap was covered by an enormous macramé bag full of knitting. Her long wooden needles were click-clacking away at a furious speed, as if the only way to prevent some impending disaster was to finish the project she was working on before she got to her station.

The train hissed to a stop. The doors opened. What looked like a full basketball team, no uniforms but carrying bags of balls, crushed its way in. Just about the biggest man that Wanda had ever been so close to ended up standing with his back directly in front of her, blocking her view of the rest of the car.

That was OK. He was black and so tall that his muscular rump was higher than her head. When she inhaled, she sucked in his musk. His incredibly baggy shorts brushed his knees. It could be that he had to wear them like that to contain an enormous dangling length. Could be.

Subways are so inspirational.

Wanda was inspired.

Seated behind that wall of flesh, she was pretty well invisible.

She knew she shouldn't, but Wanda *fantasised*.

There was no hair on the paler skin at the backs of his knees. If she were to lift a hand out of her lap and stroke that skin with her knuckles, it'd be hard and smooth and warm. How would he react to her touch? A handsome young giant like him would be used to being fondled by older women. He'd most likely chosen to stand there in front of her because, out of all the women and girls in the carriage, *she* was the one he'd chosen to be surreptitiously caressed by.

He'd twitch, but that'd be all.

Which side would he be hanging? Wanda had read, sometime, somewhere, that statistically, more men 'dressed left' than right. So if she let her fingertips glide up inside the left leg of his baggy shorts, sliding over skin that was so glossy it felt slippery ...

Oh my! It couldn't be! Could it? It was. There was no mistaking the nature of the heavy limpness that lolled against the back of her hand. If his shorts had been just two inches shorter, the head of his cock would have peeked out beneath them. What a monster!

It twitched against her hand. The young man shuffled his feet a little further apart. What more invitation could Wanda ask for? She curled her fingers around his shaft, just above its head. Their tips didn't touch. What would it feel like to have that monster invade her body? Would she be able to stretch that far?

The cock in her hand thickened and tried to lift. She grasped it firmly. It wouldn't do to embarrass the lad by allowing his erection to jut out in front of him. But she couldn't hold it down for him forever. There was only one thing she could do.

Her hand stroked, up, then down, slowly and firmly. Did he grunt? Men did, sometimes, when aroused.

The train hissed to a stop. Her new friend made no move to get out, thank goodness. Wanda pumped him again. Could she feel a pulse? He was certainly getting warmer. Better get on with it, just in case his stop was coming up. Wanda slithered her fingers up and down, sucking the sensations in through their tips. He was so *big*. He must have outweighed her better than two to one – maybe three to one – but she held him fast by the root of his power. Despite his bulging muscles, she was in control of him. The way she had him now, he'd give anything for her to continue doing what she was doing. When a man's orgasm approaches, he's nothing but a ravenous beast. That's a woman's power.

His cock was straining up, making it hard for her to hold him down. She pumped harder and faster and harder and –

Ah! There it came. She could feel the pulsing through his shaft.

It'd make a mess on the carriage's floor, but no one would know what it was, if anyone even noticed. The train stopped again. Her ebony stallion moved away to get off.

Oops! It was her stop as well. Wanda scrambled for the doors and just made it. *He* was nowhere in sight. It was best that way. If their eyes were to meet, it'd be so embarrassing. Even if she'd only fantasised their encounter, shame would be red in her cheeks. Sometimes she wondered if people could tell her dark secret just by looking at her. That too sent thrills of shame through her.

Even so, she simply *had* to stop.

Chapter Two

The Taylor Building was two blocks north of the subway station. It was a lovely day. Wanda walked it. Therapy Associates was on the twentieth floor. The receptionist had Wanda fill out a long form, though what relevance her childhood diseases had to her current emotional problems was beyond her.

Dr Sullivan would doubtless be small and slim, with a goatee and a Swiss accent. He'd wear a black jacket and pinstriped pants. Perhaps he'd have a pocket watch that she'd be asked to look at while he twirled it until she was 'under' and a slave to his perverse will. Would he ...?

'Miss Wanda Mitty? Come on in, please.'

So, he had an English or a Boston accent, she could never tell them apart, and he was well over six foot, built like a going-to-seed ex-quarterback, in a check shirt and expensive jeans. Her imagination wasn't always a hundred per cent right. The lack of a pocket watch was a bit of a disappointment though.

He sat in a big green leather chair and waved her to a smaller version of the same. His desk was a sheet of glass on spindly chrome legs. It wasn't at all the sort of desk that a girl would want to be bent over to be buggered. No doubt it was strong enough, but it *looked* flimsy and the thin glass edges would be hell on her thighs.

There was a file in front of him. He had a file on her already?

He opened it. 'I see that your mother made your appointment for you, Wanda. Was it against your wishes?'

'No, not at all. I know that I need help.'

'Pre-wedding jitters?' he asked.

'Does that seem trivial to you?'

'Getting married is life-changing. Does having concerns about it seem trivial to you, Wanda?'

'No.'

'Then it doesn't to me. Is there anything about your upcoming nuptials that worries you in particular?'

'Um.'

He waited for her to say more and, when she didn't, he asked, 'Tell me about your young man, your fiancé.'

'He's big, about your height but not so ...?"

'Bulky as me?'

'If you like. He's very good looking, charming, fastidious ..."

'Financially?'

'Very well off. There are no worries there. Oh – and he

draws, I've been told, though I haven't seen his work yet.'

'He sounds well rounded, then.' He glanced down at his file. 'Does the age difference bother you?'

'Not at all – in fact, I like it that he's a bit older. It gives me a feeling of security and it's just a bit naughty, now that I think of it. I kind of like "naughty".'

'He seems just about perfect. So?'

'Should I give you some background?'

'Excellent idea.' He picked up a pen.

'It's sort of an arranged marriage, but not exactly.'

Dr Sullivan nodded.

'That doesn't mean that I don't love him.'

'Of course not.'

'You see, my mother got into genealogy. A lot of people are, what with the Internet making it so easy. There was something in our family history that'd always fascinated her.

'Our ancestors were Puritans who settled in Oregon – mixed farming. They did OK, I guess, until the two brothers who'd inherited the farm, Henry and William, had a falling out over a servant girl.'

Dr Sullivan nodded as if he'd been expecting exactly that information.

'One night, Henry took off with all the portable valuables, including the cash, and the girl. William searched for him, in vain. As it happened, Henry had only gone fifty or so miles, across the border into Nevada. He set himself up with the family money in the corn business and changed his name to Chandler. Not much imagination, you see.'

'What's your fiancé's given name,' the doctor asked.

'Henry. Why?'

'How's his imagination?'

'I don't know.'

'I see. Go on.'

'It seems that, as well as buying and selling corn, Henry cooked and distilled it. He made a lot of money, which he invested in land, at first. Later, in all sorts of good solid things, like banks and railroads. He became a pillar of the community, a church elder, all that kind of thing.'

'And the other brother, William, your direct ancestor?'

'He went broke. He tried publishing and was unsuccessful. For a time he was a travelling carpet salesman, failed at that, then got a job on the railroad, walking the line. William was industrious enough but a bit absent-minded. He got run down by a locomotive; but not until after he'd married and fathered two sons to continue the line.'

'So one side of the family prospered while the other suffered?'

'I wouldn't say "suffered" but we were never wealthy.'

'And then your mother found Henry's mother, and they got together?'

'And became mutually obsessed with healing the family rift, using me and Henry as the glue.'

'Does he seem to resent that?' the doctor asked.

'He seems genuinely in love with me.'

'Seems?'

'Henry isn't very demonstrative.'

'Tell me more about him. What does he do?'

'He sits on boards. He's a lawyer but he doesn't practise that. He's on the committees of several charities, two churches, an orphanage, a private girls' school, plus he administers the family trust and runs the family businesses.'

'Very respectable, then.'

'*Very.*'

'Too respectable?'

How to answer that? Best say nothing.

Dr Sullivan prompted, 'He's ultra-respectable, and you?'

Fuck, he'd got right on it. Well, what would you expect from a shrink? She blurted, 'I gave my virginity away when I was quite young.'

He nodded.

'I have a healthy appetite, that way.'

'I see. And you suspect that he doesn't?'

'There's Puritan blood in the family.'

'On both sides,' he said. 'The original Henry wasn't so respectable, from what you've told me.'

'My Henry wears dark three-piece suits.'

'Is that a problem?'

'All the time? I bet he's even got three-piece chalk-striped pyjamas.'

The doctor smiled at that. 'You haven't actually seen his pyjamas yet, then?'

'No.'

'The physical side of your relationship?'

'Zero. A few kisses, but not *real* kisses. My mother warned me, when she took me to visit for the first time, "No bad language. No flirting. Don't dress sexy. Be respectful and respectable."'

'But you haven't always been so respectable, in the past?'

'You better believe it, Doctor.'

'You're sexually experienced, then; adventurous even?' He waited in vain for her to respond. 'And you don't want to give up the lifestyle you've learned to enjoy? I'm not judging you, Wanda.'

She nodded.

'How are your concerns manifesting themselves? I take it that you haven't complained to your mother that you see a less than exciting intimate life ahead of you?'

'I have, actually. She's no shrinking violet herself. She says I'll just have to teach him how to please me.'

'What do you think about that?'

'Nervous. Unsure that'd work.'

Dr Sullivan tapped his chin with his pen. 'And the immediate effect?'

'I fantasise, Doctor.'

'Sexual fantasies? About your fiancé?'

'Sexual, yes: about Henry, no.'

'There's nothing wrong with that.'

She blurted, '*All* the time. I forget things, miss appointments, don't feel safe driving.'

'Obsessive fantasies, then?'

'Yes,' Wanda admitted. 'Obsessive.'

'Then perhaps our first goal should be to bring your imagination under your control. If you control your fantasies, they can't control you. You could establish boundaries.'

Wanda nodded. It was fascinating how he seemed to be shrinking fifty or so pounds and growing a small beard.

In a slightly Germanic accent, he asked her, 'How about masturbation?'

'Yes please.'

He got out of his chair and came around to where she sat. With his left arm resting on the back of her chair, he plucked her skirt up her thighs with his right hand and slid his fingers higher, to the gusset of her panties. It was eased aside. A satisfyingly thick finger worked up into her and started pumping. Would it be polite to offer him a handjob in return or was what he was doing simply a part of her treatment?

His voice, slightly raised and with that Boston accent again, said, 'Wanda!'

'Yes, Doctor?' She blinked and he was back in his chair, back the way he had been.

Very quietly, he said, 'You were drifting off into a fantasy, weren't you?'

'Sorry.'

'No problem. Did you hear my advice?'

'Advice?'

'I asked you to keep a journal of your fantasies, totally uncensored, and bring it in with you the same time a week from now. Can you do that for me? Then we can discuss specifics.'

Yeah, and then he'd jerk off while he read them and he wouldn't even let her watch. She said, 'I can do that, Doctor. Thank you.'

A chime sounded.

'That's our time up, I'm afraid. Try to relax, Wanda. All will be well.'

On the subway ride home, Wanda still felt needy from the doctor's interrupted attentions. She pulled her skirt up, her panties down, and touched herself to a nice little climax that was greeted by the other passengers with cheers, claps and stamping feet.

Chapter Three

Wanda woke on her back in her own comfortable bed with her sheet pulled up over her face. Or she assumed that she did. She hadn't woken in someone else's bed since she'd met Henry. Still, until she opened her eyes and pulled the sheet down she wouldn't be absolutely certain she was in her own bed, would she? She might have had an accident that she didn't remember because of retrograde amnesia – was there any other kind? You couldn't very well forget your future, could you?

Perhaps she'd been in a coma, but there didn't seem to be any wires or tubes attached to her. Could they be trying something new on her? Wireless monitoring of some sort?

A pleasant baritone said, 'And this is Wanda. She's a very special patient. We are trying some new techniques on her, very hush-hush, somewhat controversial, so you don't talk about her case outside this room.'

A variety of voices said, 'We understand,' 'Of course, Doctor,' 'Mum's the word,' and things like that.

The first voice continued, 'Note the tone of her muscles.'

Her sheet was folded down to Wanda's waist, immodestly exposing her naked breasts. She kept her eyelids as slits so that she could see but they wouldn't know that she could.

Someone said, 'Excellent.'

Someone else sighed, 'Lovely.'

Wanda resisted taking a deep breath.

'Wanda is paralysed,' the voice continued, 'but she responds to touch and seems to be thinking. Under the Electrical Brain Scanner Device, the pleasure centres of her brain show activity if she is stroked: like this.'

A firm but very soft hand caressed her bare shoulder.

'If the touch is more intimate, like this –' he cupped and compressed her breast '– her brain lights up like a Christmas tree.'

'A sexual response?' someone asked.

'Certainly. We are maintaining her muscle tone by frequent massage. That's experimental, but more radical; we theorise that the continuing sexual stimulation will eventually bring her up out of her coma. She's already responded with twitches and flexed muscles.'

A higher-pitched voice asked, 'Is she still capable of achieving climax?'

'So far, four times, for sure. Two more possibles.'

A second female voice asked, 'What will our duties be, as interns, regarding this patient, Doctor?'

'We want to expose her to as much stimulus as possible, in intensity, kind and frequency. While you are about your duties, whenever you get the chance, I want you to stop by to visit Wanda. If you have reservations, just hold her hand and talk to her. If it won't offend you, give her gentle caresses or whatever else you feel comfortable with.'

A much deeper voice asked, 'Within what parameters, Doctor?'

'Do no harm. Don't hurt her or endanger her in any way, but otherwise ...'

'Intercourse?' the deep voice asked.

'By all means. Just don't talk about it, right?'

There was a chorus of eager assurances that what happened in Wanda's Ward stayed in Wanda's Ward.

The doctor said, 'That's it for you people, for today. You can go, unless you'd like to stay here and get to know Wanda a little better?'

The deep voice said, 'Seems like the charitable thing to do, don't it, Doc. I'll gladly give up some of my free time to help this poor girl.'

Apparently, he wasn't the only Good Samaritan. They all declared their willingness to tend to poor Wanda. The doctor left. There was a click, as of a door locking.

Someone folded her sheet down to her feet, leaving her naked and ashamed.

Six faces swam into Wanda's restricted view. Even paralysed, she managed to focus.

To her left, standing beside her head and holding her hand gently, stood a man who might have stepped out of just about any cop show on TV. He was of mixed Caucasian and African blood, with a shaved scalp, a neck that was as wide as his head and deltoid muscles that formed 45-degree angles with his incredibly broad shoulders. Wanda decided that his name was 'Don'. No – 'Dan'. That suited him better.

Dan said, 'I wonder if what they've tried so far has all been tactile?' He leaned down over her, lips close to her ear. 'Wanda, baby, you're such a tasty piece of ass, I'd like to smother you in whipped cream and lick every last drop off your sweet white skin.' He finished with a quick but strong lap at her nipple.

'Or how about taste?' he continued. 'Taste can be very evocative.'

'Taste of what?' Eve, a tall skinny platinum blonde, asked, with a trace of a giggle in her voice.

'This.' Dan turned Wanda's head towards himself and lifted her upper body closer. A quick tug at the drawstring at his waist dropped the pants of his scrubs to the floor. Men in shirts and wearing nothing below had always struck Wanda as kind of endearing, vulnerable but dangerous, like lions playing at being cute.

Anticipating, she relaxed her jaw. His thumb pulled down with gentle power. The juicy plum of his giant penis nudged her lips and was inside the welcome wet embrace of her mouth. He was right. Tastes are evocative. The sensations of everyone she'd ever sucked, not that there had been many, in fact, far too few, swam up from her memory.

Eve said, 'She's in a coma, Dan. She's not going to give you a blow job.'

'That's OK. I'll just leave it in there until the swelling goes down.'

'No matter how long it takes?' Eve asked.

'No matter how long. I'm a patient man.'

'I like that in a man.' Eve reached over to cup his dangling balls. 'Don't choke her, though.'

'I'll be careful.'

Meanwhile, Wanda savoured the flavour and the firm bulkiness of Dan, while striving desperately not to react with a lick or a suck. That was *hard* for a sexually deprived young lady.

The two interns at the bottom of the table, Ken, with dyed blond hair, and Barbie, with a fluffy ponytail, lifted Wanda's legs and set her knees over their shoulders, the right over Barbie's left, the left over Ken's right.

That was a blast from the past. She hadn't fantasised about sex with Ken and Barbie for a *very* long time. Two sets of fingers explored her, one male, one female. Her outer lips were palpated and then teased apart. Two fingers entered her, side by side.

'She's reacting, if getting wet counts,' Barbie announced.

17

'Try a lick, one of you,' Dan suggested. 'Oh – OK, both of you.'

Patrick, a skinny and tattooed kid who barely looked old enough to be an intern, groped below Wanda's elevated bottom and found the knot of her rectum with a fingertip.

'Good idea,' Barbie encouraged. 'That always turns *me* on.'

'You like a finger up your bum?' Patrick asked.

'Doesn't everyone?' Barbie straightened, abandoning Wanda's pussy, twitched her hips towards Patrick and dropped the bottoms of her scrubs.

Looking into each other's eyes, Barbie and Patrick reached behind and worked a finger up each other's bottom.

Fuck, it was turning into an orgy. Wanda didn't mind that, even if it meant that she was no longer the centre of attraction on her own. She was proud of not being a selfish lover, which reminded her of the last intern ... Betty Lo. Half-Chinese, small and very intense but with a childlike innocence about her. She was ... playing with Wanda's nipples, admiringly, wonderingly, as if they were the first nipples she'd ever encountered. Well, they were rather nice, of course. Perfect cones, but with flattened tops, almost always erect and very resilient. Wanda liked to have them played with, but a bit rougher than Betty's careful caresses.

18

Dan said, 'Give 'em a bit of a pinch, Betty. Make sure she feels it.' He rocked a little as he spoke, gently fucking Wanda's mouth. That wasn't exactly just leaving his cock in but Wanda didn't blame him. Her mouth was, after all, irresistible.

Once more Dan made a suggestion. He was definitely in charge. 'Ken, why don't you fuck her now?'

'Bum or pussy?'

'Maybe we could find a way to do her both ways at once? Not many girls can sleep through a three-pronged fucking.'

Eve said –

'Wake up, sleepyhead,' in Wanda's mother's voice.

Wanda eased her hands up from between her damp thighs, careful not to let the sheet over her expose what she'd been up to with her fingers. 'Mm?'

'Brunch today, remember? With Henry and Lucinda?'

That was right. Today they'd have brunch with her fiancé and his mother, her mom's best friend. That'd be nice, wouldn't it? Wouldn't it? Maybe, if she could keep her terribly lewd imagination under control.

Chapter Four

Her mom sent Wanda back to change three times. Each time it was for shorter heels, longer skirts and more modest tops. Damn it! Henry had been kept busy working on some sort of business merger and she hadn't even seen him, let alone had any private time with him, for almost a month. She really deserved a chance to turn him on a little. Even her make-up was toned down at her mom's insistence.

'The Chandlers are a prestigious family,' she said, often. 'Decorum is de rigueur.'

Wanda hated to admit it but her mom was a prude and a snob, very old school. At least, she was where Wanda was concerned. For herself, short skirts or ones with slits and less than modest necklines were fine. Not that she couldn't carry it off. Parked in her very late forties, she still had the body of a twenty-year-old.

The outing was a chance for Wanda to wear her engagement ring. It had nine diamonds, set in a square pattern of three threes. She didn't know much about gems but each stone had to be at least a carat, so the ring was too much for the supermarket. For a swanky restaurant, it was fine.

Although The Captain's Table's brunch was a buffet; the maître d' greeted Wanda and her mother and showed them to their table, where Lucinda was waiting, alone. The elegant woman, as slender, lithe and tight-skinned as Wanda's mom even though she had to be at least five years older, rose to embrace her. The two mature women air-kissed to both sides, then pecked each other's pursed lips. The contact was brief but, Wanda felt, electric. Were her mom and Henry's doing the horizontal? Wanda shuddered and thrust the thought away. *Those* were images she certainly didn't want sneaking around inside her head, waiting for their chances to soil her fantasies.

Wanda had a seat on a bench against the wall, under a cartoon of a bare-breasted mermaid riding a seahorse, side-saddle, of course. Wanda took the seat that'd be directly to Henry's head-of-the-table right. Lucinda sank into the seat that'd be to his left, between him and Wanda's mom.

'Henry's sorry he's late,' Lucinda explained. 'He's picking up his cousin, Kitty, who will be joining us.'

'Kitty?' Wanda asked.

'They've been playmates since they were children,' Lucinda continued. 'Best pals forever and all that.'

Playing what? Doctor? That wasn't a very charitable

thought. Wanda shoved it away to join her nasty suspicions about Lucinda and her mom. Kinky fantasies starring herself were bad enough. If she started involving friends and family, that'd be *really* sick. Too sick to even tell Dr Sullivan about?

Leggy waitresses in musical comedy versions of sailor suits brought champagne and orange juice. Wanda sipped and then swallowed. It was early in the day for alcohol, but a Buck's Fizz barely counts, right? Then again, she'd skipped breakfast. She pushed the flute three inches further away, then pulled it back. What the hell! She deserved *some* fun in life.

Lucinda turned her head towards the entrance and brightened. 'Here he is!' she sighed in a tone most people would have reserved for the Second Coming.

Despite herself, Wanda found that she was straightening and pulling her tummy in. He was only a man, after all. He might be six-foot four, ruggedly handsome and charming, with a boatload of money, but he was still human. Right?

Henry was wearing navy espadrilles, crisp white pants, a smart blue blazer and a cravat, and he held a captain's cap under his arm.

'Henry always likes to dress up,' Lucinda boasted.

Does he? Did that mean that he was metrosexual, or simply gay? Was he planning to marry her just to be his 'beard'?

22

Kitty, her black hair in a pixie-cut to match her big-eyed pixie-face, also wore a blue blazer, with a mid-thigh white pleated skirt, bobby-socks and deck shoes. *They* were co-ordinated. *She* wasn't. Kitty was showing her legs off. *She* wasn't.

With a great effort, Wanda stopped grinding her teeth. She rose into Henry's warmish embrace and cheek-kiss.

Lucinda made the introductions.

Henry declared that he was famished and suggested they raid the buffet. Good idea. Food would give Wanda something to sink her teeth into, apart from Kitty's elegant neck.

Henry was right in front of her in the line. He took lots of raw oysters so Wanda did likewise. So did Kitty.

'Oysters, huh?' Kitty remarked.

Not sure what the girl meant or was implying, Wanda just nodded.

'You might want a lemon wedge,' Kitty prompted her.

'I was hoping for lime,' Wanda replied, trumping the reminder but still taking the advice.

Kitty ignored that and said, 'I was hoping for some tongue. I'm very fond of tongue. How about you, Wanda?'

'That depends,' Wanda replied, leaving off the 'whose tongue' that had almost sprung to her lips.

'You're right. It certainly does depend, on so many things.' Kitty gave Wanda a brief fluttering wink, which

Wanda interpreted as 'whose tongue' plus 'and where it's licking'.

Perhaps the girl wasn't such a bad sort, after all. She was more slender than Wanda, which meant she was a bit skinny, of course. It was impossible to tell about her tits, under that blazer and a horizontal striped boat-necked cotton sweater. Wanda suspected that her own were better, or, at least, bigger.

The buffet line started with lobster tails. Wanda chose one that was arched high out of its split shell, like it was struggling to be born. There were a variety of pâtés, herring, shrimp, crab and lobster. Wanda took a serving each of the crab and the lobster. A blob of Russian salad and a few black olives absolved her conscience about taking all the high-cost, high-protein offerings, so she was able to feel fine about the two paper-thin slices of very rare roast beef, with creamed horseradish.

Henry dropped a couple of gigantic butterfly scampi on top of her beef. 'These are very good,' he told her.

'Thank you, Henry.' She could always skip supper, and breakfast tomorrow. Maybe lunch, as well.

Back at the table, a heaped bread basket plus little pots of dressing and drawn butter had appeared. Kitty shed her blazer and dropped it onto the bench seat beside her, though a waitress whipped it away in less than ten seconds. Her sweater was skin-tight so that Wanda could see that she had cup-cake tits, small but firm and projecting, with obvious nipples. Not bad. The hem of the sweater was cropped and elasticised, leaving a three-inch band of bare tanned skin at her midriff. Neither Lucinda nor Martha, Wanda's mom, showed any sign of disapproval, whereas, if it had been *her*dressed like that, she'd have been given a slow verbal roast in hell for it. Perhaps it was because Wanda was 'spoken' for and Kitty wasn't? That'd be some compensation.

Kitty nudged Wanda with her thigh. 'I'm sure that we are going to become great friends,' she declared. 'I can feel it already.' She rested a warm palm on Wanda's knee and squeezed.

'Thank you.' That was confusing. It isn't fair when someone you've decided to hate comes on all warm and friendly. And 'comes on' to boot!

Wanda picked up a small fork and prodded at the lobster meat, not sure how to proceed. Next to her, Kitty simply plucked her tail from its casing with her fingers, dipped it in a sauce and slowly sucked at the pinkish-white meat. There was no doubt in Wanda's mind. The girl was fellating the firm flesh.

Kitty dipped again. 'I *do* love this sauce, don't you, Wanda?'

'I've tasted better.'

'Haven't we all! I wonder if this is a cock or a hen lobster?'

'Does it make a difference?' Wanda asked.

'They're both good, I'm sure, but I like to know what I'm putting in my mouth, anyway.'

The blatant innuendoes confirmed that Kitty was definitely a naughty girl. Wanda liked that, even if the girl's freedom to be openly bad made her jealous. Under different circumstances, she and Kitty could have been very good friends. Come to that, she really couldn't hold Kitty's past whatever-it-had-been with Henry against her.

Henry had his head back, pouring an oyster into his mouth. His Adam's apple bobbed. Did oysters evoke the female essence for him as much as lobster tails did the male one for her?

Her mother and Lucinda were looking into each other's eyes as they too slurped oysters. Oh my God! If that didn't confirm exactly what Wanda didn't want confirmed, what would?

So as not to mimic Kitty, Wanda picked her tail up and sank her teeth into it. The sweet meat was resilient enough she could almost fancy it was alive and moving inside her mouth. On her tongue.

This wasn't a brunch. It was a goddamned food orgy!

Four loud and burly young men brought plates that were pyramided with the buffet's offerings to the next table. Wanda threw a glance at Kitty to see if she disapproved of the newcomers as much as she did. There was something about the young woman's profile ...

Wanda twisted on her bench seat and looked up at the

cartoon. There was a definite likeness between Kitty and the mermaid. And Henry drew. As far as she could see, the picture wasn't signed, not even with initials. If it had been, and the signature had been 'Henry Chandler', or the initials 'HC', that would have been *very unpleasant*.

Henry's knee touched hers under the table. Was his hand going to follow? Please?

He asked her, 'Do you ride, Wanda?'

She nodded. Her mother had made sure that she was raised 'above her station'. Upward mobility had been the theme of her life, imposed by her sole parent. Her mom hadn't been mistaken though, after all, all being well. From shoe-shop assistant to the wife of a multimillionaire would certainly be an upward move.

'English saddle, or Western?'

'Either – both. Not at once.'

He grinned, warming her heart. 'Funny girl! My negotiations will be finished in a couple of days. I plan to take a few days off to get to know my bride better.'

Did he mean sex? Please, God, let him mean hot sweaty, maybe kinky, sex!

He continued, 'I thought we could all go out to the ranch, kick back, take it easy, with maybe some riding? You have a quality about you, Wanda, that makes me want to see you in full English riding regalia.'

The men at the next table were laughing raucously.

'I don't have ...' she began.

'No, of course not. Here, take this.' Henry handed her a business card. *Mr Pink, Bespoke Habits.* 'He does boots, as well. I'd like you to go see him and let him measure you. I've told him exactly what I want him to make for you. He makes all my riding clothes for me.'

'Oh, thank you, Henry.'

'Pink doesn't do Western outfits, though, so take this as well.' He put a black credit card on the table. 'There's no practical limit on it, so don't worry about what you spend.'

Wanda had some vague impression that there was something special about black credit cards. Henry was giving her a taste of what being married to a very rich man was like. That was a kind of courtship, wasn't it? Wanda tucked both cards away in her purse and made sure to wedge her purse between herself and Kitty, where no one would be able to snatch it. The backs of Wanda's fingers pressed briefly against Kitty's hip. The hip pressed back. Wanda clamped down on her imagination before it could take her where she didn't want to go. Perhaps she should get away from the table, and the heat of Kitty's slender young body.

'I'm up for dessert,' Wanda announced.

Henry laid a finger on her wrist, where it seared her flesh. 'I hope you don't mind but I ordered a special dessert for us. It'll be right along.' He lifted his other hand, sending a waitress scurrying towards the kitchen.

'What is it?' Martha asked.

'Figs.'

Martha looked taken aback, which was exactly how Wanda felt. Figs?

Henry explained. 'Fresh green Smyrna figs, slit open and some of the pulp scooped out. They're filled with raw Demerara sugar that has been supersaturated with dark 180-proof rum. Then they are wrapped in foil and baked so that the aroma penetrates the flesh.'

Kitty, under her breath, whispered, 'Penetrates the flesh.'

Wanda couldn't help but echo, 'Penetrates the flesh.' She and Kitty exchanged sly glances and didn't giggle.

Henry continued. 'Once they are out of the oven, they are opened, topped with clotted cream and served very quickly, while the hot and cold still contrast. I think you'll find them amusing. If not, there's an ample dessert buffet to choose from.'

'I've never heard of that dish,' Wanda admitted. 'What's it called?'

'I haven't named it yet. If you like it, perhaps it will be "Figs Wanda".'

'*Your* recipe?'

'The chef here allows me to dabble.'

Oh! He likes to dress up. He cooks fancy desserts. Please, please, please don't let him be gay!

The chef himself appeared, complete with his high hat and check pants, and served them each with a single cream-slathered fig in a cut-glass coupe. Henry thanked him. He bowed to the table and retreated to his domain.

Wanda picked up her dessert fork. As she prodded through the cream, a perfume that could have got her drunk just from breathing deeply burst up at her. She dug in and scooped a morsel out. Oh! It did things on her tongue, soothing things, but exciting things. Her sinuses seemed to sigh. Beneath her tongue, saliva pooled. Wanda sucked in a deep breath. It tingled all the way down into her lungs. Perhaps deeper.

'How do you like it?' Henry asked.

Everyone but Wanda proclaimed their approval. She was too busy enjoying the contrast of texture between clotted cream and tiny smooth fig seeds. Eventually, she managed to breathe, 'Divine!'

Kitty added, 'Devilishly so! Figs *Diablo*?'

For a while, the table was quiet as all devoured Henry's creations. That seemed to make the noise from the other table louder. There was a squeal of chair legs on hardwood as one of the oafs twisted round to glare at Henry.

'Hey, you, sailor boy! You got four fine-lookin' bitches there and we got none. That's no fair! Send 'em over to us and we'll show 'em how real men treat their women.'

Henry dabbed at his lips with a napkin, set it down carefully and stood up. 'I suggest that you and your friends pay your bill and leave.' His voice was soft and calm.

'Oh yeah?' The hooligan snatched his glass beer mug up and cracked it down on the edge of his table, leaving a glittering multi-bladed weapon in his trembling fist.

Wanda stood in fear for her fiancé, though what she could do was beyond her.

The man swung shards of glass at Henry's face. Henry brushed it aside with his left hand and looped his right fist up and over to slam down on the man's cheek, driving him to his knees. He swayed, then toppled to lie there, face distorted, eyes closed, blood trickling from his nose and bubbling from the corner of his mouth.

Henry looked at the man's three companions. 'I repeat, I suggest that you pay your bill and leave.'

The three looked at each other sheepishly. One said, 'George was drunk.'

'And so are you,' Henry observed. 'And now George is on the floor.'

The three tossed bills onto the table. Two of them lifted George by his armpits and dragged him out, followed by the third.

Wanda wrapped her arms around her hero's arm. 'That was *magnificent*,' she told him.

Lucinda, Martha and Kitty all added their praise, but it was Wanda who got to hold him close. Under his sleeve, his arm was massive and unyielding.

The maître d' bustled up to their table. 'I am so sorry, Mr Chandler. I had no idea they were already drunk

31

before they came in. I'll ban them from the premises, of course.'

'Not your fault,' Henry assured him. 'Better clear their table and take care of the broken glass, right?'

'Of course! Immediately!' He hustled away.

Wanda said, 'The least he could have done after that incident is comp you our meals, Henry.'

Martha laughed. 'He couldn't very well do that, you silly girl. Henry owns this restaurant. He won't be given a bill.'

Henry fixed Wanda's mother with a look that Wanda hoped would never be aimed at her. 'Martha, unless someone had told her, how could Wanda be expected to know that? In other circumstances, she'd be absolutely right. It would have been totally appropriate.'

Martha looked down, blushing. She mumbled something that might have been an apology to Wanda.

What a man! He tackles hooligans without blinking and he defends her against her mother, a much more courageous feat. How could a girl *not* love a man like that? And, as for doubting his masculinity, how utterly ridiculous that was!

Chapter Five

After brunch, Henry had a meeting. Martha and Lucinda decided to take in some art galleries, or so they said, between giggles. Wanda had her suspicions. Kitty was at a loose end and obviously hinting, so Wanda asked her if she'd like to help her shop for Western gear, for the upcoming long weekend. It turned out that Henry's childhood friend knew exactly where to shop for stretch-fit jeans and denim short-shorts, plus a couple each of clinging micro- and hobbling-tight maxi-skirts that she promised would 'drive him crazy with lust' when combined with check shirts that tied to leave her midriff bare and high-heeled Western boots.

'How does Henry look when he's "driven crazy with lust"?' Wanda asked Kitty, nervous about the answer.

'You'll see,' was the calm reply. 'He doesn't go all red and slobbering, like some men, but you'll see it in his eyes, if you haven't already.'

'So you've seen what he looks like "in heat"?' Wanda asked.

Kitty slapped Wanda's rear. 'No need to be jealous, Wanda. He and I have double dated, not as a couple but as the other halves of other couples, if you get me.'

Wanda nodded, unsure.

'You didn't think he was a virgin, did you?'

'Of course not.'

'And nor are you, right? Sauce for the goose, as they say. Anyway, not to worry. I've seen him look at you in ways I've never seen him look at any other woman. I could almost envy you.'

'Why don't you?'

'He's my cousin, silly!'

'You two wouldn't be the first cousins ...'

'Nor the last. Let's change the subject. Do you have your trousseau picked out, yet? I'm sure that there's lots left on that credit card.'

So they shopped for undies that Wanda was going to have to hide from her mom, though, once she and Henry were married, it'd only be *his* approval she'd have to worry about. Wanda treated Kitty to a couple of things, mainly because the girl didn't so much as hint that she expected it.

She found that she warmed to Kitty, even though ...

She blurted, 'My mom seems to think that Henry is very conservative in his ways. Is that true?'

Kitty pondered. 'In some ways. You don't know him that well, do you?'

'No. It's been kind of a whirlwind courtship. We haven't had a lot of time alone together yet.'

'All the more fun exploring each other's little ways once you're married, then.'

'I hope so. I really hope so.'

'Cheer up. Time for a cocktail before you have to go home?'

'As I'm out without my mom for a change, I've time for two!'

Wanda felt sure that the slightest hint from her would have had them in bed together that very afternoon, but that, no matter how tempting, would make her life far too complicated. Still, if her worst fears about Henry proved correct, Kitty would make a lovely consolation prize. Henry had proved his masculinity but that didn't mean that he wasn't the stuffed shirt that her mom seemed convinced he was.

When she got back to the apartment she shared with her mother, her mom'd had at least a couple of cocktails herself, so Wanda was able to smuggle her secret purchases up to her bedroom. Let sleeping moms lie. There was a huge carton sitting on her bed. Wanda loved presents. She tore the box apart like a lion tears at an antelope, or, it occurred to her, like a very horny woman tears the pants off her lover.

She uncovered a giant teddy bear. It stood tall enough to come up to her nipples when its hind paws were on the floor. There was no doubt that it was a female bear. Its silky plush fur was pink. It had upswept eyelashes that were a good two inches long, a pink bow on top of its head and a tiny pink tongue that poked out between its ursine lips.

It couldn't have a male name, so it wasn't 'Teddy'. Wanda decided that she'd call it 'Edwina', which she'd then abbreviate to 'Teddy'. Obviously, it was not only female, it was also a lesbian bear. That'd be much more fun.

Wanda went downstairs to check on her mom. She was still asleep on the couch with a silly grin on her face. Wanda covered her with a throw, had a quick goodnight gin and tonic, and went back up to shower.

With her mom fast asleep downstairs, it was OK for Wanda to leave the bathroom naked, still towelling herself dry. One day, she hoped, she'd do the same in front of Henry. And he'd approve heartily. Of course he would. For him, she'd dance with her towel serving as a fan-dancer's fan, or she'd even prance like a pony, like this ... She high-stepped, pointing her toes, twirling and skipping to amuse her husband, her lover, her friend.

Oops! She was fantasising again, but this time *about Henry*. That was new. Did it mean that she was making progress? She'd have to ask Dr Sullivan when she saw him.

Edwina, 'Teddy', was waiting in Wanda's bedroom, sitting up in the old rocking chair. Wanda bowed with a flourish, flinging her towel aside.

'Lovely body!' the bear told her in a deep but certainly feminine contralto.

'Thank you, Teddy. I only have one bed, I'm afraid. Do you mind if we share? No? Come on, then. Oh – and I don't have any nightclothes that would fit you, Teddy, my dear. Still, it's just us girls, so that's all right.

Wanda's was a double bed but Teddy was quite bulky so they had to snuggle close, face-to-face. Wanda said, 'Goodnight, Teddy,' and pecked her bear on the lips. That, of course, poked the animal's tiny pink tongue between Wanda's lips. She'd assumed it was made of some sort of fabric but it didn't feel at all like cloth. It felt like some sort of rubbery material, complete with a texture that mimicked taste buds.

Hm.

Wanda kissed again, a little sucking kiss. Teddy groaned appreciatively. Unfortunately, the way her toy had been made, really deep kisses weren't possible, but tongue-tip to tongue-tip was nice, in a teasing sort of way. Wanda snuggled in closer. Teddy's left leg flopped up over Wanda's right leg. A furry right leg insinuated itself between Wanda's smooth thighs. Plush tickled Wanda's tummy. She wriggled, drawing her bear in even closer. Furry pubes pressed against peach-fuzz ones. Wanda gave a little bump. Teddy, perhaps helped by Wanda's hand on her rump, pushed back.

This wasn't a fantasy, Wanda reminded herself, apart from the way she interpreted the bear's growls. This was, however, being honest, masturbation, using an inanimate object. Women used vibrators. That wasn't considered aberrant anymore. Even so, Wanda suspected that fucking teddy bears was still considered a bit kinky, at the least. Never mind. Dr Sullivan would sort the pros and cons out for her.

Teddy growled.

'Sorry, I was distracted.' Wanda sucked Teddy's little tongue and ground her hips hard against her new lover.

Tongue? Wanda experimented by pulling Teddy's head down to her breast and rubbing that rubbery nub on her nipple. It felt nice, and when Wanda pushed Teddy's head back, her legs slid further between Wanda's. Wanda pressed the bear's shoulders away and wriggled down even harder. The animal's right leg came right up to divide Wanda's breasts. Her left leg stuck up along Wanda's back. Wanda reached behind herself to grab a hind paw. Her other hand took hold of the other furry ankle. When Wanda pulled up on the front leg, then tugged the back one, bear-pubes sawed on Wanda's pussy, squishing its lips and grinding on her clit. See-saw. See-saw. There was no penetration but the friction was certainly ... interesting. Very interesting. Very, very interesting.

Climactically interesting.

OK, so it wasn't spectacular, but it was a different way to get off. That had to count for something. Perhaps that nice little orgasm would protect her from her fantasies for a while? Whatever, her sleep that night was dreamless.

Chapter Six

Wanda woke to find Teddy with her head on the floor and her hind legs up on the bed. She pulled her new friend up. 'Teddy, how do you feel about anal sex?' It was a reasonable question to ask a bear who might well be sharing her marriage bed one day. 'Do you like to take big bare cocks up your tight bear bum?'

Teddy didn't answer, of course. Wanda giggled. It had to be a healthy sign that she could joke to herself about her problem with fantasising.

It was a busy day. First, Dr Sullivan, who accepted her twenty-two-page single-spaced printout of a week's worth of erotic fantasies without comment. He was hard to read. Wanda thought he approved of her fantasising about Henry, now, and he seemed to agree that her bear episode didn't belong on her list of imagined perversions, as it wasn't imagined. He didn't say that it was a kinky thing to do but neither did he say that it wasn't. His face was stone when she admitted to being attracted to Henry's cousin Kitty. Perhaps that was the sign of a good therapist, that the patient had no idea what was right or wrong.

Finally, Wanda bitched about it having been so long since she'd had her hands on a nice erection – so Dr Sullivan let her spend the rest of her appointment playing with his.

After lunch, Wanda headed for her sartorial appointment.

Mr Pink, Bespoke Habits, had a tiny body and a big head. If his ears had been a bit larger and pointed, he'd have been a perfect elf. He pranced around his premises so lightly that his black patent shoes barely whispered against the thick carpet. His being such a flaming queen, Wanda had no qualms about him measuring her inside leg. She had to wonder, though, how Henry felt about having the same measurement taken.

Maybe one day *she'd* measure Henry's inside leg. Both legs, to be sure. He 'dressed left' she thought. So when she measured his right leg, several times, she'd let the knuckles of her right hand run gently up the inside of his left thigh. Then she'd look up into his eyes, because he'd be looking down at her, and do it again, no longer pretending that it was accidental. He'd smile. She'd turn her hand and fondle the thickening length of his flesh through the cloth of his pants. Henry would put his hand on her head, giving her his blessing to continue. Her other hand would tug his zipper down. She'd reach in and fumble until she found his heat. His fingers would tighten in her hair. She'd pull the entire length of his magnificent erection out into the open and inspect it, carefully and slowly, making sure to breathe on it. Her lips would part. She'd lick her lips *at* him. She'd stretch out her tongue, desperate for a taste but Henry's fingers would grip tight, pulling at the roots of her hair as he prevented her from reaching her treat – and then he'd relent. Her lips would stretch wide to fit over that smooth hard dome and her tongue –

'Could you sit down please, Miss Mitty? I have to measure your head,' Mr Pink said.

Head? Oh well, she guessed he knew what he was doing. She said, 'Sorry. I guess I was daydreaming.'

Mr Pink smiled. 'That's natural, for a young bride.'

Had he read her mind?

Mr Pink was meticulous. Wanda had been measured for clothes before but never before had she had the distance between her nape and her left nipple taken, then the same to her right nipple. She tried to peek at Mr Pink's notes, just to be sure those two measurements were identical, but his fluttering hands made that impossible. When it came to her feet, not only did he measure each one's length and width but also floor-to-arch, floor-to-instep and two diameters. Those were followed by the distance around her ankles and around her calves at two different heights. Her boots, she was convinced, were going to *fit* with a capital 'F'.

How deliciously sybaritic!

'What will my outfit be like, Mr Pink?' she asked. 'What colour?'

'I have my instructions from Mr Chandler,' he replied.

'But …?

'That's all I'm free to tell you, Miss. I wouldn't want to spoil the surprise now, would I?'

Wanda felt like stamping one foot at that but Henry wasn't there to see her being cutely childish, so she didn't bother.

Chapter Seven

A stretch limousine arrived to take Wanda and her mom to the airport. Both ladies wore plain jeans and casual sweaters. As Martha explained, 'Air travel is an ordeal. It *ruins* good clothes.'

They drove right past the airport. Martha tapped on the dividing window and told their driver, 'You've made a wrong turn, young man. The entrance is behind us now. Can you turn around?'

'No, Madam, sorry. I thought you knew. That was the public airport. We'll be at our destination in a few minutes.'

Martha 'humphed'. Wanda didn't say a word. The limo turned in through tall gates and followed a private road to a small jet that was parked outside a hangar. The plane was dark green with a gold racing stripe. Ostentatious?

'Here you are, ladies,' their driver told them. 'Don't worry about your luggage. It's being taken care of.'

They were greeted by a woman – oh, it was Kitty! She was dressed as a stewardess, not a 'flight attendant', but definitely a 'stew'. Her uniform jacket was tight-waisted. Her skirt was two inches longer than her jacket. Even so, it had slits up the sides. She had very good legs, as Wanda already knew. And Wanda was wearing practical jeans. Damn!

Henry liked 'dress up'. That was fine, but it should have been Wanda dressing up to cater to his whims, not cousin Kitty.

'Welcome to Chandler One,' Kitty told them. 'This way please, ladies.'

There was a movable staircase up to the plane. Kitty went first, flirting her miniskirt with every step. Without making it obvious, Wanda tried to peek up but she didn't manage to see whether Kitty was wearing anything under her skirt. Chances were she wasn't, the little slut!

The cabin had heavy leather armchairs on swivel bases. Lucinda was sipping what looked like a gin and tonic. Wanda sat.

'No, Wanda, not there,' Kitty said. 'You get to ride up front, in the pilot's cabin.'

That seemed weird but it made sense when Wanda got there. Henry was in the pilot's seat, in a sort of uniform with wings over his breast pocket. He *did* like to dress up!

Her fiancé was talking pilot-talk into a mic the size

of a pinhead. It was all 'Wind-speed, CAT, ceiling', and similar things that meant nothing to Wanda.

He smiled at her but kept talking. His fingers flipped toggles and turned dials. The jets roared and rumbled. Henry began to ease back on the yoke. Wanda knew the name of that one from some movie or another.

'What time's take-off, Captain?' she asked, and added, to show off, 'ETD?'

He grinned and nodded towards the window. Wanda looked out. Oh! The airfield was dropping away.

'That was smooth,' she told him.

'Thank you. I try.'

Wanda took a moment to absorb all the new information. Her 'intended' had his own jet plane that he piloted himself. Every day, it seemed, she had to revise her idea of how wealthy he was, and how talented, both upwards. What next? Did he perform brain surgery on alternate Thursdays?

There was a knock on the cabin door. Kitty returned. 'Coffee, tea, or ...' She handed Wanda a Martini. 'Henry doesn't drink and fly,' she explained, 'but I find a small libation helps my nerves when he's piloting.'

'He's an expert pilot,' Wanda protested.

'Of course he is. He's good at everything he does, isn't he.' She winked. 'It's quite tiresome how damned talented our Henry is.'

'Stop teasing,' Henry told her.

'Aye-aye, Captain.'

'We won't be flying very high,' Henry said. 'It's only a short hop to the ranch.'

They entered a cloudbank. Nothing but fluffy white was visible.

Wanda asked, 'Can you see OK, Henry?'

He patted his console. '*She* can, but if you're nervous ...' He eased the yoke back and they burst into sunshine again.

'Thank you.'

'It's time, Kitty,' he said.

'Right.' The girl took Wanda's hardly touched glass and disappeared.

'We're descending now,' Henry told Wanda. He started pilot-talk again.

Wanda looked out. They had to have passed the clouds because it was clear all the way down to the ground. The landscape was pretty much shades of khaki, except that straight ahead was a patch of lush green. It seemed that was where they were headed.

'There's the ranch house,' Henry told her.

She looked out as he banked in a slow turn over a sprawling building with a red-tile roof, mainly, and stucco or adobe walls with black timbers. It was one floor, again 'mainly', but two high in some places and three where a tower stood in one corner.

'My great-grandfather built the original house,' Henry

said. 'Since then it just "grew". I don't think any architect would approve, but we like it. I hope that you do too, as it'll be your home soon, or one of them.'

'It's lovely,' she assured him. One of them? How many?

'Thank you for that. The "Bar C" thanks you, as well.'

Wanda blew a kiss at the house and told it, 'You're lovely, Bar C.'

They crossed a paddock. A dozen horses chased the plane's shadow.

'What beautiful animals!' Wanda exclaimed.

'You'll see a lot of those.'

'A lot?'

'That's what we do here, breed and train horses.'

'Oh, I didn't know. How – how much land?'

'It's not a big spread, a little over a thousand acres, but the landscape is very varied, which is ideal for our purposes. Our horses are sold to hobbyists, pets that they can ride on. We breed for looks and disposition mainly but they also have to be ready for any sort of terrain they might encounter.'

The landing strip was only a hundred feet from the house. Once Wanda alighted, the rest of the day was something of a blur. Almost everyone she was introduced to was attractive, which sent her conscious mind scurrying for cover in case her subconscious fed these people into the furnace that drove her erotic fantasies. There was the housekeeper-cum-cook, Consuela Sigurdsson, a handsome

Brazilian woman showing spectacular cleavage. She was in her fifties. Her husband, Olaf, was safe to think about, a dour little man with a walrus moustache. He was the handyman. Consuela had three helpers, all pretty young women with tight little bodies and saucy eyes. Her three sons, whose names Wanda didn't manage to remember, all looked the way cowboys were supposed to look – rangy, with no hips, tanned faces with creases around their eyes. Their jeans were sun-bleached and worn thin, particularly around their crotches. The three managed the ranch in Henry's absence. *Any* healthy young woman would have started fantasising about group sex at her first sight of them. For Wanda, it took a massive effort of will not to moisten when they each took her hand, in turn, and wished her welcome. It helped that their hands were so calloused it felt like she was shaking hands with crabs.

The eldest had breeding records he needed to consult with Henry about so it fell to the other two to help Wanda into a Range Rover and give her a quick tour of the buildings. What they referred to as the 'swimming hole' turned out to be a well-appointed in-ground pool, complete, to Wanda's dismay, with three swimmers, two muscular men in tight Speedos and a lovely flame-haired woman in a minute bikini.

Where would all this temptation stop?

Lunch was informal. There was a choice of lamb chops or pan-fried rainbow trout, with buttered potatoes that weren't much bigger than the peas they accompanied. After the meal, Henry was whisked off for more ranch business.

Kitty and Lucinda announced that they planned to get some sun that afternoon. There was a girls-only sunbathing spot on the roof. Wanda and her mom were invited.

Wanda chose a two-piece swimsuit that the saleswoman had called a bikini but had too much fabric to qualify for that title, in Wanda's opinion. When she got to the roof, her confusion was compounded. Her mom, her future mother-in-law and Kitty were all stretched out on loungers wearing just the bottom halves of what certainly qualified to be called bikinis. Wanda swallowed hard. She blushed. She averted her eyes but the images were branded under her eyelids. Seeing Lucinda's bare and obviously augmented breasts was a shock enough, though Wanda had to admit that whoever it was who'd worked on them had done a fine job. Looking at Kitty's naked little boobs might have been enjoyable, under other circumstances. Her mom's nakedness was an entirely different thing. Her breasts were nothing for her to be ashamed of, considering her age, but they were her *mom's*.

And it was her mom who said, 'You're overdressed, Wanda. Didn't you hear Lucinda tell us that this was a ladies-only zone?'

Somehow, Wanda managed to shed her bra, snatch up

a magazine, and get behind it on a lounger. *Guns and Ammo*. Not exactly her favourite reading material, but changing it for another would have meant exposing her body to their eyes, and their bodies to hers.

One of the pretty young girls brought them drinks. Was *she* going to bare her boobs as well? Thank Heaven, it appeared not.

Wanda sank down behind her magazine. Kitty was off to her left so that Wanda was able to take crafty glimpses at her boobs from behind her sunglasses. Those delectable little tits actually tilted up at their nipples. Wanda had never seen that before, not in real life, not that she'd seen that many real breasts close up.

She'd have felt a lot more comfortable if her mom and mom-in-law-to-be had left. Now, if they just decided to go down to one of their bedrooms and do whatever middle-aged lesbians did to each other, she could really relax and enjoy the sun. If they'd just get up, go through the door that led down, lock it behind them, then …

A shadow falling over her told Wanda that Kitty had come to visit.

'I've seen you eyeing my tits,' the girl said. 'It's OK. I've been dying to get a good look at yours. They're beautiful.'

'Thanks. Yours too,' Wanda assured her.

Kitty leaned over Wanda. 'You can touch them if you like.'

'I think I will.' Wanda cupped one and gave it a little squeeze.

'May I?' Kitty asked, her hand hovering over Wanda's left breast.

'Please do.'

The two young women caressed each other, stroking and compressing and then, inevitable, toying with nipples.

'I'd love to be a fly on the wall when you and Henry are alone,' Kitty said.

'You would?'

'Two beautiful bodies, doing beautiful things to each other. I'd enjoy watching that. Do you like to watch, Wanda?'

'I guess I do.'

'Henry's a very lucky man. I bet you give him great head.'

'What makes you say that?'

'You're a horny little bitch, Wanda, *you* know that. It shows in your eyes.'

'I suppose I am.'

'It's the best way, you know,' Kitty mused.

'Best way to what?'

'To keep a man. No man ever left a woman who was giving him regular blow jobs, and doing it with enthusiasm.'

'I'll remember that,' Wanda promised.

'And not always when he expects it, either,' Kitty

continued. 'Like, under his desk when he's working, or bending over his lap to do it while he's driving. Each one of those counts as two, you know.'

'It does? Two, how?'

'Well, if you're in bed and expecting a good tonguing yourself, or after he's got you off and you fancy a taste of the good stuff. Those are good, but surprise head counts for double brownie points.'

Wanda asked, 'Or if it's you and your girlfriend and you both blow him at the same time, what does that count?'

Kitty giggled. 'Four regular ones, at least, maybe five. Did you plan …?'

'Just checking on the rules.'

'You're *bad*, Wanda.'

'And wet.'

'Are you?' Kitty squirmed a hand down the front of Wanda's swimsuit bottom. 'Did *I* do that to you, Wanda? Did *I* make you all wet?'

'No one else is around, talking dirty to me, so I guess you must be to blame.'

'Are you horny, Wanda? Are you *very* horny?'

Wanda nodded.

'Lift up, then.'

Wanda raised her bottom. Kitty dragged the half swim-suit down her thighs and off.

'Spread 'em, Wanda,' the girl instructed.

Wanda spread wide and squirmed lower down on the recliner. Kitty pulled a footstool over to sit on.

'Pretty pussy.'

'Purr.'

'Pussy want a nice stroke?'

'Purr.'

Delicate fingers smoothed over Wanda's puffy mound. The heel of Kitty's hand pressed down on it, tilting Wanda's lips and parting them a little.

'You're leaking.' She sucked in a deep breath. 'Delicious!'

'Purr.'

A finger of Kitty's other hand tickled the delicate area just below Wanda's sex. 'Do you like that?'

'Mm.'

'You have to tell me.'

'I like it.'

'A lot?'

'A lot.'

'How about this?' A finger wormed into Wanda, down low, where her lips formed a little cup.

'Love it.'

Kitty leaned in closer and sucked up the accumulated dew. 'Yummy.'

'Thank you. There's lots more where that came from.'

'I believe you're right.' Using one hand to part Wanda's lips, Kitty stroked up inside the full length of her slit.

Her tongue followed, then passed the fingertips to rest on Wanda's little pink button.

'Oh yes,' Wanda gasped. 'There. Right there.'

'Like this?' Kitty lapped.

'Exactly like that.'

'Wouldn't it be fun,' Kitty mused, 'if Henry were here now, watching what I'm doing to you.'

That thought sent a massive jolt through Wanda. 'Oh, fuck, yes!'

'He could be fucking me from behind while he watched me play with your pussy,' Kitty suggested.

'I can't stand it,' Wanda moaned.

'But you have to.' Kitty's fingers formed a demanding dagger to stab into Wanda repeatedly as her tongue lashed at Wanda's clit. It was too much. The sensations, plus the mental image of Henry watching them as he was fucking Kitty, were overwhelming. Wanda felt that she was drowning in lust and then there was the sound of a deep bell that reverberated in her bones and –

'I think that's the dinner gong,' Kitty said from over on her lounger.

Lucinda added from hers, 'Time to go get changed. Dresses or skirts please, ladies.'

Chapter Eight

Over dinner, Beef Wellington with truffles and Caesar salads, Henry had apologised for being so busy and told her that he'd make it up to her in the morning. The delivery from Mr Pink had arrived. They'd go for a ride in their new riding clothes. He'd show her the property. Would seven be OK?

In the morning? Ouch. Wanda agreed that seven would be just fine, if she could get an early call.

'I'll have Sandy bring you a light breakfast and your new outfit, at five-thirty then?'

Wanda had nodded. She'd have an hour and a half to get herself fully awake and dressed. That was doable. Of course it was.

After dinner, she excused herself to go up to bed. It'd been years since she'd ridden. She'd need to be well rested. Tomorrow, she'd be spending the entire day alone with her Henry. Perhaps he intended to mount more than his horse. Wanda couldn't think of a better cure for her erotic fantasising than *real* sex.

She woke at five, ready to get up and go. By the time Sandy arrived with a gigantic cardboard box and a breakfast tray, Wanda had showered and trimmed everywhere that could possibly need trimming.

All she had on was the tiniest and flimsiest of her thongs. Wanda grabbed a bedspread to drag over her lap.

Sandy said, 'You are so beautiful, Miss!'

With that reaction as encouragement, Wanda tossed the spread aside. Sandy was pretty cute, herself, in her navel-baring short-shorts and 'tied under the ample boobs' shirt. Wanda couldn't help but wonder, with all the good-looking girls on his staff, how many of them Henry had …

She asked, 'Does Mr Henry mind the way you dress, Sandy?'

The girl smiled down into her own cleavage. 'I've had a woman or two disapprove, Miss, but never a man.' She grinned at Wanda. 'Do I offend *you*, Miss?'

'Not in the least. You have a lovely body, Sandy. I was just wondering about how they like things around here. I wouldn't want to offend anyone.'

Sandy gave Wanda a long slow look, up and then down again. 'Miss Wanda, you're gorgeous. Mr Henry is a lucky man. I'm sure he'd approve of you taking advantage of your looks. If you've got it, flaunt it, and you've got it.'

'My mother doesn't agree.'

'Oh, mothers! What do they know?'

Wanda considered that an excellent question.

There were hot croissants with fresh butter and apricot jam, plus a single fig on the side. The coffee was divine. As Wanda ate, Sandy unpacked the box. She giggled.

Wanda turned to see the girl holding up something in satin, with dark-green and gold vertical stripes – the same colours as Henry's plane. His livery? Was he somehow 'taking possession' of her? She really hoped so.

'It's a waspie, Miss,' Sandy said. 'You'll *kill* in this.'

Wanda felt a *femme fatale* mood creep up on her. A tight waspie, sheer hose, stiletto heels and a cigarette in a long ivory holder, and she'd be ready for ... What? Just about anything naughty, she supposed. Please let Henry have something 'naughty' in mind!

Wanda had to step into the waspie to save unlacing it. Sandy worked it up over Wanda's hips. Inevitably, there was some skin-on-skin contact but neither of them acknowledged it. The situation was far too fraught with possibilities.

There'd been pictures that Wanda had seen, years before, pictures that she shouldn't have looked at. If Sandy had been dressed as a sexy French maid while Wanda was leaning forward and supporting herself stiff-armed on the dresser while Sandy tightened the waspie with her knee in Wanda's back and Henry had walked in on them ... Well, the outcome could have

58

been *delicious*. He'd have been dressed for riding, of course, and carrying a crop.

A crop.

Stop! She hadn't indulged in *that* sort of fantasy for *ages*. Having those particular images in her head would have been unbearable, considering how long she'd been forced to remain celibate.

'Pull tighter,' she told Sandy. Perhaps being constricted at her waist would squeeze the dangerous thoughts out of her head. 'Tighter!'

Sandy tugged hard.

When breathing became a struggle, Wanda allowed, 'Enough! Now, what else goes with this outfit. I suppose that there *is* more to it, or am I to do a Lady Godiva?'

Sandy giggled. 'You're bad, Miss Wanda.'

She was the second person to tell Wanda that, in two days. No – the other had been Kitty, in a fantasy. Perhaps her life was going to imitate her erotic dreams? Wouldn't *that* be a blast!

The riding habit was dark-green velvet. Its skirt was ankle-length and double-circular. There was a gold silk shirt with ruffles at the throat. Neither Wanda nor Sandy mentioned the possibility of her wearing a bra under it. The short jacket had puffy shoulders but was tight at her waist and wrists. If Wanda hadn't been wearing the waspie, Sandy wouldn't have been able to get the seventeen cloth-covered buttons done up.

The boots were matching green, in supple kid leather, with three-inch Cuban heels. Wanda had to point her toes and strain on the boots' tabs to get into them but once they were on they felt like slippers.

When Wanda checked herself in the mirror, she might have stepped out of an English movie, set in the days of highwaymen and carriages.

'Your hat,' Sandy said.

It was reinforced and similar to a top hat but not so high and with a jauntily tilted crown. The long trailing ribbon was gold, of course, as was the cockade. There was no doubt, Henry was dressing her in his livery colours. Something trembled in her tummy.

'And ...' Sandy said.

Of course, there had to be a riding crop. It was made of green suede, plaited, with a leather loop for her wrist that had 'Wanda' embossed on it in gold.

How did Wanda feel about her outfit? She wished she knew. Excited? Scared? Thrilled? *Wicked?* All of those, and more.

'May I do your make-up, Miss?' Sandy asked.

The way Wanda's fingers were trembling, it was a good idea for someone else to apply her paint for her. She nodded, set her hat aside and sat at the dressing table. Sandy made her lips very red and tinted her eyelids with green and gold. The effect was a bit over the top for seven in the morning but Wanda didn't say anything.

Somehow, coming up with words seemed a bit beyond her capabilities, right then.

Henry and another of the pretty girls, Elaine, were waiting right outside the front door. Wanda's mount, obviously hers, was a stunning Palomino mare with a long almost-white tail and mane. Henry's horse was an enormous and glossy-black stallion. Her fiancé was wearing a masculine version of her hat, sans ribbon or cockade, a black swallowtail coat, a beige cravat at his throat, beige whipcord pants and black leather boots that were so shiny they looked almost transparent.

He introduced Wanda to the animals. 'Blondie, for obvious reasons, and Satan, but he's a pussy cat, really.'

'For you he is,' Sandy said.

'Blondie is your horse now,' Henry told Wanda. 'Apart from exercise, no one else will get to ride her.' He chuckled. 'Don't all the girls want ponies?'

Wanda felt like throwing herself into his arms and kissing him but not with the two girls there. Perhaps he'd let her express her gratitude more fully when they were alone. She settled for stammering a stream of 'thank yous' that didn't stop until he laid a hand on her arm.

Henry produced a camera and took pictures of Wanda before she mounted, while she mounted, with Sandy's help, and after she'd mounted.

She'd asked if he wanted her to ride side-saddle but he

assured her that wasn't a good idea if they were going to ride for long.

Wanda adjusted her skirts. It took a moment to get used to a saddle without a horn again and her naughty side insisted that there be nothing between her soft pubes and hard leather but her flimsy thong. That was part of the joy of riding, after all, that and having a great powerful beast clamped between her thighs.

'Comfy?' Henry asked, smiling.

Had he guessed what she was doing? No, of course not. That was a girls' secret, unsuspected by the opposite gender. Wasn't it?

Henry swung up into his saddle with one fluid movement. Wanda nudged Blondie with her knees. The mare ambled forward at a slow walk. Henry, on Satan, followed a few feet behind. Obviously, he was checking how she sat before they really got going. To show him that she was a capable rider, she encouraged Blondie into a canter.

Wanda soon adjusted to her mount and matched their rhythms. Every forward movement of her hips slithered her sex against hard leather. She might as well have left her thong off for all the protection it gave her. Thank goodness for her voluminous skirts. Without them, Henry might have heard the slippery sounds Wanda could feel that her pussy was making.

She'd already been shown the buildings close to

the ranch house. Henry led them cross-country, past paddocks with pregnant mares and with mares with colts. The stallions, Wanda presumed, were kept elsewhere.

As if reading her mind, Henry told her, 'We mainly use artificial insemination, but I do keep a few studs to take care of things the old-fashioned way once in a while. It seems fairer to the mares, to me.'

Wanda almost asked if she could watch, but bit the question back.

Henry's ranch seemed to go on forever, even though he'd said it was a modest thousand acres. There were streams that they jumped or waded but he didn't take her over any fences or hedges. It was nice that he was protective but she'd have liked the chance to show her skills off. Then again, what if she'd set Blondie at a tall hedge and the mare had balked? Wanda might have been thrown. She'd fallen off a horse once and hadn't come to any serious harm, but still …

Blondie would likely have taken off, out of shame, leaving Wanda without a mount. Satan was an enormous beast, perfectly capable of carrying two riders at once. Henry would have simply scooped her up and sat her before him. Her back would have been pressed against his broad chest. His breath would have been hot on her nape. That always made her shiver.

And they'd be rocking, hips forward and back, forward and back. That'd be nice, co-ordinated, but nicer if she rocked back as he rocked forward. That might send him a not-so-subtle message.

Fuck subtle!

She pushed back as hard as she could, grinding her bum against his crotch. Henry handed her the reins. His right arm circled her. The buttons of her jacket popped open as if of their own accord. The same happened to those of her blouse. That big hand took hold of the naked softness of her left breast and palpated it, the way she loved.

From the feel of it, he was unzipping his pants. Wanda sucked air, hoping she was right. His left hand fumbled up under her voluminous skirts until his palm covered her bare tummy. His little finger brushed down to find the protruding button of her clit.

It was *so* good. What next? Something kinky, she hoped.

Somehow, he pushed down on her back, forcing her to wrap her arms around Satan's mighty neck. The stallion was hot from the gallop. With her cheek pressed against his glossy coat, she could feel the ripple of his powerful muscles. She inhaled the musky aroma of horse sweat. One beast beneath her, another over her ... She was trapped between two incredibly powerful male animals and she never wanted to be free.

Henry reared up, over her. He dragged her skirts up to her waist, leaving her bare bum exposed. Somehow, her thong had been lost.

It pressed down, parting her cheeks. She relaxed those special muscles. The pressure became almost painful ... and then her sphincter parted and accepted the great dome of Henry's erection. It paused for a split second before forcing her to accept deep impalement. She was *owned*.

Satan pounded. Henry thrust. The movements syncopated, then opposed each other, crushing Wanda each time they came together. She had no choice but to surrender, body and soul, accepting the dominance of her beloved master.

Satan accelerated, heading straight for a hedge that had to be six feet high, at least. He soared. Henry pulled back a fraction while they were still in the air.

And Satan thudded onto turf, safe and sound, but that final deepest impalement drove Wanda's poor body into the most powerful orgasm she'd ever experienced.

Henry, riding Satan beside her and her mount, said, 'You really gave Blondie a workout there, Wanda. You're quite the horsewoman. You have an excellent seat.'

Seat? Did he mean ...? Of course not. He couldn't know what she'd been fantasising about, could he?

She said, 'I'm getting a bit peckish, Henry. Are we far from home?'

'Can you last another two miles?'

'Of course.'

'Come on then.' He galloped ahead. She cantered after him. Wanda was too drained to gallop.

Two miles took them to a stream that widened into a pond with an impressive weeping willow drooping over it. There, beside a spread-out rug, was a cooler and a great big wicker picnic basket. How on earth had that come to be?

Henry helped her off Blondie and led her by her hand to sprawl on the rug. Their mounts ambled over to the pond to drink. Wanda supposed that Henry knew what he was doing, leaving the horses untethered. He *was* a horse trainer, after all. If they ran off, she hoped he'd give her a piggy-back all the way home.

'There's vichyssoise, three kinds of pâté, some cheeses, a chicken, cold cuts, garlic potato salad, fruit, crackers, butter and fresh baked bread, from Consuela's kitchen.'

'In the cooler?'

'White wine, champagne, sangria and various pops and waters.'

'We're here for the week?'

'That'd be nice. Here, see what you think of this.' He reached over and held a cracker piled with creamy pâté to her lips.

Wanda lifted up to prop herself on stiff arms. She knew the pose suited her. As she nibbled on the treat, she talked with her eyes, looking straight at Henry, hoping he'd interpret her steamy look correctly.

For a quiet half-hour, he fed her tidbits and sips of wine. Wanda moved her shoulders closer, to emphasise her breasts. Judging from his downward glances, the manoeuvre wasn't wasted.

Henry drained her glass for her and set it aside. Wanda, anticipating, lay back flat. His face loomed above her. It was the nearest she'd seen it from. It passed close inspection. He leaned in closer. Firm but gentle lips brushed her. Wanda resisted the urge to slip her tongue into his mouth. That initiative was his, the first time. Once the benchmark had been passed, she'd feel free to take the lead. In Wanda's mind, that was the way with all sexual activities. Once he'd fondled her tits, she'd be justified in guiding his hand to them, when that was what she fancied, which was most, if not all, of the time. The same, or similar, went for intimate fondling, fucking, oral play and anal. Once Henry opened those doors, they'd be permanently unlocked, both ways.

Door one?

He nibbled on her lower lip. She relaxed it, parting her lips slightly. There was a hand on her jacket, flipping buttons undone. He'd been faster in her fantasy. That couldn't be helped.

With each button that surrendered to his touch, his nibbles became more forceful. As he brushed her jacket open, his tongue, *finally*, slid into her mouth.

Was this it? Was this the beginning of the rest of her life? Their wedding day would be a milestone, for sure, but if he 'seduced' her here, now, that would be their true first union. She *had* to make sure that they continued to consummation.

She kissed him back, putting all the passion she could into it. His mouth was cinnamon and honey. When his hand passed the barrier of her blouse and cupped her breast, she moaned into his mouth. Daring, she reached behind him, hooked her fingers into the waistband of his pants and pulled him fully on top of herself. He squeezed her breast. She sighed. He gave her nipple a little pinch; she gasped and humped up at him. With this much encouragement, no man could retreat. Her thighs spread. Should she steer his hand up under her rumpled skirts? Would tugging his zipper down be more effective? Before Wanda could decide, something buzzed.

Henry lifted up, with a sigh and a 'Damn!' He produced a cellphone from somewhere. 'Yes?' His face went cold. 'I see,' he said. 'Very well.' He put the cellphone away.

'Emergency,' he told Wanda. 'We have to go back. I have to be in London by ten in the morning, their time.'

Chapter Nine

Despite the delicious sweetbreads, whatever *they* were, for dinner, Wanda was in inner turmoil. Henry had actually started making love to her, which was a long-overdue thrill. Their passion had been interrupted, by business. Business. Damn business! Damn Henry for letting business get in the way.

Now she was furious, on one hand, and so horny her teeth ached, on the other. Once she'd seen Henry off in his jet, she started into Beefeater martinis, accompanied and encouraged by Kitty. The thought of bedding her fiancé's pretty cousin passed through her mind once more. *That'd* teach Henry to leave her hanging, not that he'd ever know, of course. It'd also slake her lust. She'd already done Kitty, in fantasy, so doing her in real life wouldn't be that big a step, would it?

But she loved Henry. Damn it! She really *loved* the bastard!

By ten, her face was glowing and the tips of her

fingers were numb. That meant, stop drinking. She had just one more, slurred her 'goodnights' and staggered up to bed.

In nothing but a short T-shirt, she snuggled under the bedclothes on the gigantic Mexican-style four-poster. By habit, Wanda's hands were between her thighs. She toyed with her pussy's lips, wet her thumb and slipped it on her clit, worked two, then three fingers up inside herself, but nothing worked. She tried imagining how it would have gone if that bloody cellphone hadn't gone off. That didn't work. Replaying her penetration-on-horseback fantasy did no good, either. Perhaps it was the booze. Maybe it was the conflict between lust and anger. Whatever it was, Wanda drifted off to sleep without the benefit of an orgasm.

And she dreamt.

There were voices coming from the big old red barn. One was male, and stern. The other was girlish, and pleading. The gargantuan doors were ajar. Wanda crept between them, leapt a moat that was filled with hairy crocodiles and landed on springy wooden planks. Chaff billowed up around her. When it cleared, and when her eyes adjusted to the dim light, she was on one side of a stack of hay bales. The people she'd heard were on the other side. One was Henry, terrifyingly masculine in his boots, pale jodhpurs and bare-chested. The other was Elaine, dressed as Wanda had last seen her, tight micro-shorts and a check shirt tied under her buxom chest, presenting them more than covering them.

Henry said, 'You trained Blondie. Blondie threw my beloved Wanda. I'm holding you responsible. What do you have to say for yourself?'

Elaine snivelled and begged for mercy.

'Perhaps it is *you* who needs further training,' Henry suggested.

Elaine nodded and allowed, 'Perhaps.'

'Turn.'

Elaine turned her back to Henry. His big strong hands took hold of the collar of her shirt and ripped it in two, effortlessly. Ruined fabric slithered down her arms to drop on the floor. He hooked his fingers into the waistband of her shorts, at the back. Those too were rent and discarded. The girl stood naked, one arm across her breasts, the other hand shielding her pubes.

'Assume the position,' Henry told her.

She bent over a sawhorse, her upper chest resting on the rough wood, chin beyond it, arms extended to the sides, legs straight and spread. With a few deft movements, Henry bound the girl's arms to the crossbar, rendering her helpless.

Damn, but Elaine looked good like that. Her breasts were hanging free, showing themselves to the best possible advantage. Her slender legs guided Wanda's eyes up past her shapely thighs, to the cleft peach of her delicious bottom.

Was Henry going to fuck Elaine? Was *that* to be her punishment? If so, Wanda planned to commit some sin at the first possible opportunity.

But no. Henry produced a willow switch, likely cut from the tree they'd picnicked under. *That* was more like a punishment. Dream-Wanda, still in only the short T-shirt she'd worn to bed, put her hand to her own sex. Getting off to this sort of scene would be a really wicked thing to do. That made it all the more tempting.

Henry swung. Elaine yelped. A red line blossomed across the girl's bottom, crossing both cheeks. Henry's arm drew back but before he could deliver another cut, as it can happen in dreams, Wanda became the one bent over the sawhorse and Elaine was hidden somewhere back in the hay, spying on the scene.

Naked, bent over, legs spread, Wanda felt thrillingly exposed. Delightfully helpless. Those emotions came from the part of her that she didn't think about if she could help it. The dark Wanda.

She'd show the little bitch how a real woman takes a good switching! Yelp at the first blow, huh? Watch *this* and learn!

With Wanda as his subject, Henry's approach changed. He came close and reached under her, to her pendant breasts. His manipulations of her flesh were firm enough to threaten but not so harsh as to really hurt. His other hand stroked her flanks and smoothed over the left cheek of her bum, much as she'd seen Henry caress a pony. His hand dropped to her leg, just above her knee, and fondled its way up to the very top of her thigh, close to the lips of her sex.

He cupped her sex and squeezed. She felt her nectar run into his palm. He lifted his hand to his lips. Henry *liked* her liquid lust. She was deeply aroused. Was that shameful or something to be proud of?

He said, 'You understand that I have to discipline you, Wanda, don't you?'

'What did I do wrong?'

'Nothing. This isn't a punishment. It's discipline for its own sake. You understand?'

'Yes, Henry.'

'You'll be brave?'

'I'll try.'

'I know that you will. You remember your words?'

There'd been an article in *Cosmopolitan*, so Wanda knew to say, 'Green, amber, red.'

'Very good. I know that you will endure all you can but there is no shame, when it gets too much, to let me know. Understood?'

'Thank you, Henry.'

He stroked her bum, compressing and releasing, seeming to enjoy the resilience of her flesh. That was nice but the anticipation of pain made her shiver.

'Please, Henry?'

'Please what?'

'Start?'

'Are you impatient for it?'

'Anticipation is hard to take.'

'Exactly. That's part of it. Sometimes, I might make you wait all day, or longer.'

'I couldn't stand that.'

'You'd have no choice.'

'No, Henry, I wouldn't. That's how it should be.'

'Good girl.'

His words were barely out of his mouth when she felt the first slash of the willow switch, across the backs of her thighs just above her knees. Wanda sucked air but she didn't cry out. Gentle fingers explored the welt she felt was rising. He squatted and traced the line with the tip of his tongue. In a strange way, it was an incredibly *intimate* caress. Having her man lick the wound he'd inflicted was an experience most women would never get to enjoy. Wanda felt privileged.

He stood. She braced. The next blow fell an inch higher, quickly followed by a third, fourth and fifth. The shock of the rapidity of those cuts brought tears to her eyes but Wanda bit her lip. One foot came up off the ground as her leg bent in a protective reflex. She forced it back down. She would stand fast. She wasn't going to struggle or cry out, no matter what.

'Beautiful,' he said. 'I'm so proud of you.'

Wanda glowed. This was what she'd secretly dreaded and lusted after for a long, long time. Her fear had been that she wouldn't be strong enough to endure the pain. Now it was happening. She was proving herself. Those hairy crocodiles would have to accept defeat.

When Henry started striping the cheeks of Wanda's bottom, he alternated each stroke of the switch with long slow caresses. It was almost as though he could read her soul through the Braille of her welts. Flowers of pleasure-pain blossomed and spread ... She could feel her own arousal dripping down the insides of her thighs. The sensations were agonising bliss. Even so, the pain was at her threshold. Wanda knew that, if she had to endure just a few more blows, she'd disgrace herself by crying, 'Red.'

And he stopped. He told her, 'I'm very proud of you, Wanda. You are a brave girl.'

That alone made all that she had endured worthwhile.

Wanda heard his zipper hiss. A hand steadied her on the small of her back. His erection nudged the lips of her sex. There was no resistance. Her body would have sucked him in, if it could. His shaft moved into her at a tantalising pace. It seemed to take forever before she felt the fabric of his jodhpurs press against her burning thighs. She was *full*.

He withdrew just as slowly, all the way out, so that she was totally void for eternal seconds before he made contact and fulfilled her once more. In deep. Out. In deep. His rhythm slowly accelerated until he was pounding furiously, heedless of her punished bottom. His arm wrapped around her. His fingers found her clitoris and strummed. His other arm reached up to caress the back of her neck and slide into her hair, where it became a fist that drew her head back mercilessly.

Wanda made little yelps. She had no choice. All self-control had left her. *He* commanded her, body and mind and soul. Flames of liquid lust engulfed her loins. She climaxed, once, twice, three times. During the inner convulsions of her third joyous explosion, she felt the flood of his male essence sluice into her most convoluted depths.

When Wanda woke, at dawn, her hands were still knotted between her thighs. They were sticky with her spending. There was no soreness or stiffness in her lower body. One day, she swore, there would be. That would be a glorious day.

Would it be as a result of Henry's ministrations? She hoped so, but now she'd tasted the perverse pleasures of corporal punishment, even if only in a dream, if Henry failed to provide them for her, she'd simply have to find someone who would.

Oh! Had she really thought that?

Chapter Ten

Wanda lay in. Consuela sent a tray up but Wanda just nibbled at the bacon. There were tumultuous emotions she had to deal with, all inspired by her depraved dream. Did she or didn't she want those terrible things in real life? If she did, what did that say about her? She'd known she was naughty for a long time but that sort of sex was beyond 'naughty'. It was downright *bad*.

Still, enjoying pain and discipline in fantasy didn't mean that she'd like it in reality. Or that she wouldn't, come to that. Her laptop was in a drawer beside the bed. She'd record it all, in every shameful detail, and let Dr Sullivan sort her feelings out for her.

Lunch was an assortment of quiches, including one that was very garlicky, made with escargots, and a delish Waldorf salad.

Kitty asked Wanda, 'Are you going to try the escargot quiche?' When Wanda shook her head, Kitty declared that, in that case, neither would she.

That was interesting. When it was 'both of us or neither' for a garlic dish, it signalled imminent kissing, didn't it? As if to confirm the notion, the mothers polished off that aromatic quiche between them.

When the cock is away, the hens will play?

The hypocritical mothers declared that they were off to the 'swimming hole' for the afternoon. The way they said it, they weren't asking Wanda or Kitty for company. There'd be cowboys at the pool, Wanda assumed. If not, the mature women always had each other. Wanda was slowly getting used to the idea that her mother was not only a cougar, but she was also bisexual. It was nice that she still enjoyed sex, at her age, but she really should afford Wanda the same privilege, at hers.

As soon as Lucinda and Martha left the room, Kitty said, 'I want to work on my tan. I'd love you to join me, Wanda.'

She'd 'love her to'? That seemed significant.

'We could let our hair down,' Kitty continued. 'Really get to know each other. Dish the dirt, no holds barred.'

That thought was a tad intimidating, but also very tempting. Wanda nodded and said, 'Ten minutes?'

'Fifteen.'

With no moms to worry about, Wanda chose one of her sexiest bikini bottoms. The catalogue had called it a 'dental floss'. The name indicated that the back was no more than a single strand, worn *between* the cheeks, leaving them totally bare. In this case, the front didn't cover much more. Wanda had been saving it for her honeymoon, but, to punish Henry, she'd wear it for the first time when she was alone with Kitty. Was that tempting Kitty, and fate? Perhaps. So? Kitty was here for her. Henry wasn't. If 'something' happened, it would be on Henry's head.

What did she mean by 'something'? Wanda decided it was best not to think about that. *Que sera sera!*

When Wanda went through the door to the sunbathing area of the roof, Kitty was already there, in a bikini bottom that covered perhaps twenty-five per cent more of her mound than Wanda's did of hers. There was an ice bucket on the table, with three large bottles of wine cooling.

Kitty looked Wanda up and down and said, 'Yummy.' She dragged a metal chair to the door and wedged it under the doorknob. 'We don't want to be disturbed, do we? Not by *anyone*.'

Wanda nodded, poured herself a glass of sparkly wine and took it to the same lounger she'd used before. Kitty took *her* same lounger, but it'd been moved. Now it was beside Wanda's, parallel, not eighteen inches away. It wouldn't be like they were sharing a lounger for two, but close to it. Kitty swallowed half of the contents of her glass and saluted Wanda. She said, '*In vino veritas* – there's truth in wine. It'll oil our tongues so that we can *really* get to know each other, *intimately*.'

How obvious a 'come on' was that! Wanda took a sip of wine and openly admired Kitty's pert little tits. From the movement of her eyes, Kitty returned the compliment. They really should start to chat before the tension grew much more, but Wanda loved erotic tension so she decided to wait Kitty out.

'You must be really suffering,' the young woman finally said.

'Suffering?'

'Frustration? I'm no Sherlock Holmes but I know that you were called back early from your ride with Henry. Your hair was mussed. You had no lipstick on, even though your eyes were made up. Your jacket wasn't buttoned right and your shirt hung out below it. Henry's lips were much redder than usual. It all adds up to *coitus interruptus* – making out that *didn't* come to a happy ending.'

Wanda shrugged. 'What's a girl to do?'

'Masturbate?'

Wanda tried to look shocked but a giggle escaped.

Kitty reached under her lounger and pulled something out of her beach bag. It was ten inches of fluted plastic with a smooth lopsided head. How should Wanda react to *that*? When in doubt, look blank. Kitty obviously misunderstood the look.

'It's a vibrator – a toy cock.'

'Oh?' Best to play dumb and see where Kitty was headed with this.

'It works,' she was told. 'Unlike some real cocks, it never fails to get you off.'

'I see, I think.'

'This is a new one, just for you. I brought it just in case.'

'In case I was frustrated?'

'I know Henry and business. There's always a chance he'll go flying off, leaving a girl in suspense.' She poured another glass. 'Do you …? Would you …? I can show you how it works, if you like.'

Kitty had such a puppy-dog expression that Wanda almost laughed. It had taken Henry's cousin a lot of courage to get to this point. It wouldn't be nice to deny her acting out what seemed to be a fantasy that was important to her. Funny, with all Wanda's erotic dreams, she'd never had one about watching another woman masturbate. This was different. As a rule, she fantasised about things that she'd never done but fancied. This would be a first for her – doing something for real that she'd never rehearsed in her mind.

'Is it difficult?' she asked, wide-eyed.

'Not at all.' Her face fiery with embarrassment, Kitty dug into her bag again. She produced another vibrator, identical to the one she'd given to Wanda. 'One each.'

'So you'll show me and I copy you?'

'If you're up for it.'

'I wonder if I am?' Wanda mused. 'Why don't we try it and find out?'

81

'Am I shocking you?' Kitty asked, frowning.

'Not yet. You can try to, if you'd like.'

'We can't do it properly with our bikini bottoms on.'

'I suppose not. You first.'

Kitty, gazing across the narrow gap into Wanda's eyes, tugged on the bow at her hip. The bitch took her time, pulling an inch, then two, then on the other loose end. Finally, the bow unravelled. The skimpy covering flopped, halfway exposing Kitty's mound. It looked to Wanda as if the girl shaved it, or something. The baldness didn't make her look any the less feminine. Perhaps more so.

Kitty lifted up, swiftly tugged the other bow undone and tossed her bikini bottom aside. 'There,' she said. 'That's me, absolutely and completely stark naked.'

'You're beautiful,' Wanda told her.

'Thanks. Your turn.'

Two can play at teasing. Wanda hooked her thumbs into the sides of her thong and pushed down on the right, then the left, peeling fabric off her mound a fraction of an inch at a time. Kitty bit her lower lip. When all that held the fabric in place was the cling of her pussy's lips, Wanda raised both legs up high, toes pointed, posed for a second then bent her knees and whipped the garment away from under herself in one smooth motion. It dangled from one toe until Wanda flipped it aside.

'And that's me, also naked,' she announced.

'Ready?'

'Nervous, of course,' Wanda lied, 'but as ready as I'll ever be.'

'These vibrators have two speeds,' Kitty explained. She demonstrated by twisting the base of her toy. 'Start slow, till you can't stand it, then fast when you go for the finish.'

'That makes sense. You promised you'd show me.'

'It works best if you think about something sexy.'

Wanda made a show of letting her gaze wander over Kitty's body. The girl arched in response, spreading her ribcage like an erotic fan, lifting those cute little breasts to point her nipples skywards.

Wanda asked, 'Do I need to, when I'm already looking at something *very* sexy?'

Kitty's eyes widened. 'You like me "that way"?'

'Who wouldn't? If I wasn't engaged to your cousin, I'd have been all over you by now.'

'Oh. Now it's you who is shocking me.'

'In a bad way?'

'Not at all. I just didn't realise. I've been lusting after you since we met at that brunch.'

'Mutual.'

'What are we going to do about it, Wanda?'

'Right now, you are going to teach me how to use a vibrator.'

'Doing that, looking at each other while we both masturbate, you don't count that as cheating on Henry?'

'We aren't touching, are we? Sisters get to see each other naked, don't they? Even sisters in spirit?'

'While masturbating?' Kitty lifted an eyebrow.

'I wouldn't be surprised, knowing some sisters. So, when does this lesson start, Sis?'

Kitty rolled onto her back with her knees up and spread her thighs far apart. She turned the vibrator on low and ran its head from just above her right knee all the way to her groin.

'I can't see,' Wanda complained.

'Sorry.' Kitty rolled to her side, facing Wanda. Her left knee stayed lifted. Her right leg drooped off the lounger.

Wanda followed suit. With just eighteen inches between the loungers, their dangling legs were perilously close, but not actually touching. That's all that counted, right?

Kitty repeated trailing her vibrator up her leg. Wanda imitated her. It was interesting to get the chance to take a close look at another girl's pussy. Wanda had only seen one before, and the light had been dim under the sheets. Kitty's lips were a bit crinkly, where Wanda's own came together smoothly. The wrinkles weren't unattractive. It made them very feminine and perhaps a little more mature-looking than Wanda's.

Kitty stroked those lips, where they met, with the tip of her toy. Pretending it was her first experience of that inanimate caress, Wanda did the same, and shivered. The shiver wasn't put on. She'd done it before, with a similar plastic penis, but never with a very pretty girl watching her.

The lips of both pussies began to thicken and part.

'Nice?' Kitty asked.

'Mm.'

'Now we tease ourselves.' Kitty drew the head of her vibrator up along the crease of her left groin, dawdled it across the lower curve of her tummy and down the right crease.

'That feels nice,' Wanda said as she copied.

'Try this.'

Kitty applied the shivering plastic to her mound, just above where her sex's lips met, and pressed.

'Oh yes! I do like that! I can feel it all the way ...'

'To your clit? Inside your quim?'

'Quim?' Wanda asked.

'It's English for pussy. It's a word I learned when I was on vacation in London last year. They're a kinky lot, those Brits.'

'Travel is broadening, I've heard,' Wanda said.

'Oh yes, the museums, the art, the theatres, all very mind-expanding.'

'And the sex?'

'I learned a thing or two.'

'That you'll teach me?'

'That's complicated. Let's wait and see, OK?'

'OK.'

Kitty was running her toy up and down the crease where her pussy's lips met. They sighed apart as they engorged. Wanda felt that her own were doing the same.

'Do we put them inside us?' she asked.

'Are you ready for that?'

'I'm just following your lead.'

'Wherever it takes you?'

'Like you said, "Let's wait and see."' Meanwhile, let's turn the volume up, shall we?'

The slow penetration tensed Wanda's legs, so that her dangling foot rose. Its instep fitted neatly into the smooth warm curve of Kitty's arch. It felt good. They'd agreed 'no touching'. Wanda thought about that. A foot caressing a foot didn't count as really them touching, did it? If not, how about ankles? Knees? Thighs? Thigh-rubbing-on-thigh would *definitely* count as touching, so it was a slippery slope. Wanda had lots of willpower. She could limit herself to just foot contact. Of course she could. Easy.

With her foot definitely caressing Kitty's, Wanda followed the girl's lead by feeding plastic into herself low, where her sex's lips met, then drawing it up to press on the underside of her pubic bone. Oh yes!

Kitty husked, 'When you get to the head of your clit, you have to experiment a bit. It's too intense for me, right on the button, so I fold my lip over, like this –' she demonstrated '– and lay the vibe alongside, to my left. That way, it's exactly right, and after a little while … A little while …' Her voice deepened. 'It. Begins. To make. Me. Oh yes. Make me. Oh, fuck, Wanda, I can't stand … You're so lovely! Come with me, darling. I love you! Come with me!'

Kitty knotted at her belly and shivered. Wanda increased the pressure she was putting on her own clit. It'd be nice if they did climax simultaneously, though not vital.

Kitty arched up and virtually did the splits. Wanda tried hard to get *there* but her orgasm came after Kitty's by a good ten seconds. Oh well, next time, maybe.

Exhausted, in a very nice way, Wanda flopped onto her back. There was a flash of light from the tower in the far corner of the ranch house. She told Kitty.

'Oh fuck!' was the response. 'There's an old telescope up there. It belonged to Henry's dad. It's ancient but pretty powerful. Someone's been watching us.'

'Hell! Who? I mean, who do you think?'

'I don't know but I know how to find out and, when I do, *someone* is going to be very sorry.'

'So we can't do this ever again?' Wanda asked.

'Sure we can. Anyway, this isn't the only private spot in a thousand acres. Don't worry. I'll take care of the spy.' She paused and frowned. 'Wanda?'

'Yes?'

'What I said, back then …'

'About loving me?'

'Let me explain ...'

'No need. I love you too, Kitty, as a sister.'

'Good. I didn't want there to be any misunderstanding.'

Wanda levelled her gaze at her newly intimate friend. 'I think we understand each other very well, Kitty, don't you?'

Chapter Eleven

That night, while the moms watched game shows on TV and Wanda and Kitty read, Kitty passed Wanda a note. That made Wanda nervous. What would she do if it was a declaration of undying love? It'd be flattering but damned awkward.

In her bedroom, she read it.

Wanda, I have hatched a devious plot. Tomorrow, at breakfast, announce that you are going to spend the morning sunbathing again. It doesn't matter if the moms offer to join you. I will myself, later. If you are alone, just put on the best show you can for our Peeping Tom. When I come up, I'll knock 2-1-2. I'll explain later.

Affectionately, your new Sis, Kitty-Kat.

P.S. Destroy this note.

Wanda tore it up and flushed it. 'Curiouser and curiouser,' as Alice would have said.

Come morning, she did as she was bid. The moms needed retail therapy, so they'd be driving to the nearest shopping mall, which was an hour and a half away. Taking that into consideration, Wanda took her new vibrator up with her. That'd help further Kitty's 'devious plot' most likely, and, in any case, there was something about being watched while masturbating that was quite appealing. Would whoever it was masturbate while spying? It seemed likely. If he or she didn't, it'd be a bit of an insult, wouldn't it?

On the roof, in her 'slingshot' one-piece, Wanda blocked the door as Kitty had shown her how to do. She was wearing sunglasses so she could secretly watch the tower but no flashes showed so far. Her swimsuit, that wouldn't be safe to swim in, was little more than a pouch for her pubes and two straps, each about two inches wide, to stretch over her nipples and link behind her neck. It was secured by a thin tape around her waist, tied with a bow. Striptease music would have been appropriate but she'd manage to put on a show without it. Kitty was *fun*! Wanda had never realised how good it would be to have a partner in crime. At least, not one who was a girl.

She arranged her lounger to give the best view to anyone in the tower and set the vibrator close at hand in an unspoken promise to her secret observer. There was a bar-sized fridge in the corner. She bent to search it, aiming her bum at any potential Peeping Tom. From behind, she'd look naked. There was wine, pop, water and ice in the fridge. Wanda filled a small plastic bucket with ice and selected a Lime Perrier.

Sprawled on her lounger, Wanda contrived to 'accidentally' brush the strap over her right breast aside. She pulled it back up but so sloppily that it slid off again.

Was the Peeper watching? He'd likely be a tall cowboy, his Stetson pushed back out of the way, his shirt off because he'd been working so hard. He'd have a rangy body, all whipcord and leather, with broad flat pectorals that bore tiny dark, and hard, nipples. There'd be a thin line of black curls from his navel down to his pubic hair. Pubic hair? Oh yes, he'd have pushed his jeans down to his knees. As he gazed through the telescope at her, he'd be slowly stroking up and down the full length of an erection that was so hard it quivered.

Wanda licked her lips. Her right hand fumbled an ice cube from the bucket. Its chill bit into her naked nipple, making hard flesh even harder. Exaggerating her response, Wanda arched up from the lounger and bit her lip. Another cube. Brush the other strap aside. Torment both nipples at once. Gasp! Pant a little. Now both cubes to her right nipple, pinching it between them. By then, it was so chilled it barely felt the torment but Wanda's face showed as much lust as she could contrive.

91

What next? Should she use the vibrator? Was the unknown voyeur ready for that, or should she tease some more? One thing was sure. If he was watching, as she and Kitty suspected, she'd give him his money's worth and for long enough that his stroking would become frantic and he'd come hard and strong.

Teasing was so much fun!

More ice in each hand. The right covered her right breast and massaged the fistful of cold into her skin. Her left …? Her left hand dripped ice-water in a trail down to her pubes and dug under the tiny pouch that barely covered her mound. When she poked a melting cube between the lips of her sex, Wanda jerked for real. That was *cold*!

She was hotter. Wanda could feel the ice melting and cold water filling her until it overflowed and saturated her slingshot where it held her most delicate flesh. It felt weird, but nice, even though her clit was chilled to total numbness.

She'd remember this for when she finally got to play with Henry. 'Darling, please chill my clit with ice, till I can't feel it, then warm it up with your mouth and tongue.' Frozen fingers always tingled painfully when they defrosted. It'd likely be twice as bad when it was her poor clit that felt the blood-flow return.

There she was, imagining the perverted pleasure of pain again. What *was* wrong with you, Wanda? What would Dr Sullivan think of this?

What was she? Fantasist? Masochist? Both voyeur and exhibitionist. Bisexual? And she'd enjoyed being laced up tightly in that waspie. Was that another kink? And her Teddy? Damn, she was a one-woman catalogue of perversion. How could she stand to live with herself?

While there was still ice in her pouch, Wanda put the plastic toy down there. With her clit so numb, it felt kind of weird. She felt the vibrations in her pubic bone more than anywhere, and yet her horniness level was rising. She bore down harder, right on her clit, which she wouldn't have been able to stand if not for the ice. It still felt like almost nothing was happening but suddenly Wanda experienced flow and release, just like a climax but without the jolt of joy. Interesting. Live and learn. Experiment and experience. She resolved to never turn down trying new ways to enjoy sex, except for the yucky ones, of course.

What next? How to hold the voyeur's interest now that she'd already climaxed? Fake something? Somehow, that seemed distasteful.

There was a series of knocks, two, one, two. Kitty! That solved her problem. Wanda unbarred and opened the door. Kitty slipped in wearing a man's shirt that she was holding together. Wanda spread her arms for a hug but her friend shrugged her shirt off first, leaving herself in just a pair of the stretch denim shorts that Wanda had treated her to.

Kitty closed the hug before Wanda had a chance to adjust, with lots of skin-on-skin and some unnecessary wriggling.

'We should kiss,' Kitty whispered into Wanda's ear. 'You know, for the watcher.'

'Uh-uh. I'm being faithful to Henry, remember.'

'Until you marry him, at least. Fair enough. It's a complicated line you are drawing between what's "allowed" and what's "taboo", but it's *your* line. Let me be straight with you, Wanda, sweetheart, sooner or later I'm going to get into your panties, so resign yourself to it.'

'*Que sera sera.*' Wanda had qualms. She was hetero, right? Mainly? Being so horny and doing without for these past months had made her vulnerable, and Kitty was a very attractive young woman. Perhaps Wanda had led the girl on, just a bit? When it came down to it, though, she was in love with a wonderful, if frustrating, man. Once their marriage was being consummated on a regular basis she wouldn't need or even be interested in sex with other people. Right? Right! She'd better redraw that line. It'd be fairer to Kitty, who seemed to be crushing on her.

'Do you think it worked?' she asked. 'Was my performance fruitful or in vain?'

'Oh, you were watched, all right.'

'How do you know?'

'The door to the tower is locked, from the inside.'

94

'Tell me, then! Who is it?'

'I don't know yet, but we'll soon find out.'

'Grrrr! You are *so* frustrating, Kitty.'

'If you're frustrated ...' Kitty reached for Wanda.

Wanda skipped back a step. 'Lookee, lookee but no touchee, no feelee, remember?'

'And you call *me* frustrating?' The girl looked at the wet patch on Wanda's lounger. 'Oh boy, did you ever –'

'It's ice. Melted ice, that's all.'

'Of course it is.'

'I don't do that ... squirting thing.'

'I could teach you how,' Kitty offered, 'but I'm a "hands on" teacher.'

'Will you stop it? Now, do you or do you not know who the Peeper is?'

'I don't know who it is but I soon will, all being well.' Kitty skinned out of her shorts and lay down, vibrator in hand. 'That's all I'm going to tell you for now, so don't be a bug, please, OK?'

'I can be patient,' Wanda lied. 'When will you know?'

'Soon.' Kitty turned the base of her toy to 'on' and parted her thighs. 'Now, if you don't want to play, I have some pent-up lust to discharge. You're welcome to watch me, or our Peeper can get an exclusive.'

'Fuck!' Wanda, uncharacteristically, said. She sat on her own lounger, avoiding the wet spot, and said, 'As I'm already here, carry on then. Do it.'

95

Chapter Twelve

Lunch was a surprisingly tasty cream of carrot soup, game pie and an anise salad, with apricot crêpes for dessert. As it was just Kitty and Wanda at the table, Consuela didn't offer any alternatives. Wanda was dubious about the game pie's cold jelly-set contents but her first bite sufficed to dismiss her reservations. Pheasant, venison and hare? She'd never tasted any of those before but she certainly would again. And the rich jelly was 'to die for'. She resolved to ride Blondie that afternoon. If she didn't start exercising more, she'd blimp up, for sure.

There was a message from the moms. They'd scored theatre tickets and would be sleeping over in town for a couple of nights. They could be reached at the Hilton, suite 1112. Kitty giggled. Wanda threw her friend a 'look' but couldn't help giggling herself. Just one suite for the two of them? That was a dead giveaway, if ever there was one.

Wanda was contemplating a second crêpe when they heard raised voices from the kitchen.

Consuela said, 'I don't care if that's some sort of crazy new fashion, go and wash your silly face.'

A masculine voice replied, 'Why, Ma? I showered this morning, like always. I'm clean.'

Kitty's foot nudged Wanda's under the table.

Consuela continued, with steel in her voice, 'Don't argue with me, boy, go do it, *now.*'

Chuck, Consuela's youngest, trudged through the eating room, head bowed and shoulders slouching. He glanced quickly at the women, then away, his face crimson with shame.

Once he'd left, Kitty said, 'See, Wanda? When I set a trap for a man, he's caught.'

Wanda asked, 'What? How on earth did you do that?'

'I ringed the eyepiece of the telescope with eyeliner.'

'So that's why he looks like a raccoon! Kitty, you are one crafty little bitch!'

'Aren't I now! You saw how red his face was when he realised we'd heard his mom give him hell? How red do you think it'll be after he looks in the mirror and finds out why?'

'So you've caught our Peeper. Now what are you going to do with him?'

'Let the punishment fit the crime.'

'Meaning?'

'You'll see.'

When Chuck came back through, he tried to be invisible,

which is hard for six-foot two of lanky ranch-hand.

Kitty stopped him in his tracks with a sharp: 'Chuck, we need to talk. On the side veranda, twenty minutes, got it?'

He nodded and swallowed hard.

When he got to his unwelcome appointment with Kitty and Wanda, he was full of false bravado. 'You can't tell Mr Henry on me,' he said. 'I'd tell him what you two was up to.'

Kitty replied, 'Mr Henry? I wasn't thinking of telling him. He wouldn't care, anyway, but he'd sure fire your ass, young man.'

'What then?'

'How would you like your mom to know that you spy on Mr Henry's lady guests?'

The boy went paper-white and clutched the hitching rail. 'Y-you wouldn't!'

Kitty narrowed her eyes. 'Maybe, maybe not. It depends. Chuck, if you want to save your miserable skin, I *own* you. You got that?'

'W-what do you mean?'

'You'll see. I say "frog", you jump, got it?'

He nodded.

'Frog.'

He did a little jump.

'More enthusiasm, next time. Now, these are my instructions. Tomorrow morning, nine o'clock, report to the roof sundeck. Don't be late.'

'I ain't allowed out there.'

'Only the three of us will know. No excuses. Be there.'

'Yes, Miss,' he told Kitty. 'Yes, Ma'am,' to Wanda.

'You may leave us.'

He actually bowed as he backed away.

'Got him!' Kitty said.

'So, what will you do with him?'

'You'll see, my sister in conspiracy. You'll see, tomorrow morning.'

'I don't get even a tiny hint?'

Kitty mused. 'Very well, just one.'

'And that is?'

'There will be ice involved.'

That gave Wanda food for thought as she rode Blondie that afternoon. Some of the ideas she came up with she hoped *weren't* what Kitty had in mind for Chuck, but who knew? The girl had a wicked streak as wide as a football field. She might be capable of just about anything, given a helpless male slave to torment. Being someone's slave could be very dangerous, with the wrong mistress – or master. With the right one, on the other hand ... Wanda shivered deliciously, despite the warmth of the day. The words 'To love, honour and *obey*' echoed in her mind. She and Henry hadn't discussed their vows yet. She somehow thought they never would. Henry didn't seem the 'discussing' kind of man. He seemed more the arbitrary-decision type. She'd heard it said that the best possible form of government would be a truly benevolent dictatorship. It made sense to her.

Then again, there'd been no mention of a prenuptial agreement. The day they married, she'd become a very rich woman, not that the money was relevant. Of course not. No way. She'd still marry him if he was broke, for sure. Not to disrespect wealth, though.

She nudged Blondie into a gallop so that she'd have to concentrate on riding and force her imagination to rest. Wanda rode hard until her thighs were as stretched and stiff as she hoped they'd get on her honeymoon, or even sooner, Henry willing.

At a quarter to nine the next morning, Wanda, wearing a brief summer play dress and ballet flats, made her way through the ranch's formal dining room. Its furnishings were antique mahogany. She thought they were Duncan Phyfe, but she wasn't sure. The table had ten chairs along each side, so, with Henry at the head and her at the foot, it'd seat twenty-two. Most likely it was only used for high days and holidays. There was a floor-to-ceiling serpentine breakfront that was really impressive, if a little overbearing.

The next room held linen chests and shelves of flatware and glasses, handy for the dining room. In the far-left corner there was the wrought-iron spiral staircase that Kitty had told her led up into the tower. The next floor was for storage, mainly plain, handmade pine furniture. It had to be from the original ranch house. Wanda couldn't imagine how the heavy pieces could be manoeuvred down the spiral stairs, but that wasn't her problem.

The top floor had big round windows on all four sides. There were a couple of armchairs and a bookcase that was full of dusty old books. A side table held a humidor that was empty. Close at hand was an ashtray stand and a small cabinet that had likely held booze at one time. This room had to have been Henry's grandpa's private retreat. What had he used the telescope for? Star-gazing or peeping at lady guests? She'd never know. Some of each, maybe?

The telescope was more modern than she expected. It was thick, with two barrels, and it wasn't 'telescopic'. It had no brass rings. That silly boy, Chuck, had left it aimed at the sunbathing roof. Well, that saved her from adjusting its position. Wanda tore open a wet-wipe pack and very carefully cleaned off the make-up Kitty had smeared around the eyepiece. The lad had moved an armchair to the perfect position. Wanda sank into it and put her eye to the 'scope. Half a turn of the lens brought the rooftop into perfect focus, just in time for her to see Kitty, in a minute crocheted pink bikini, let Chuck into the men-forbidden area and wedge the chair under the door's handle.

Wanda couldn't hear what was being said on the rooftop but Kitty seemed to be accommodating her for that with theatrical hand gestures and movements. With one hand fisted on her hip, she pointed to Chuck's boots. He kicked out of them sheepishly. Kitty wagged a finger under his nose. He stood at attention and went red as she unbuttoned his shirt and pulled it down off his broad shoulders. Kitty walked around him, inspecting his chest, shoulders and back, like he was livestock she might be persuaded to buy, if the price was right. Chuck's lower lip quivered with embarrassment. Showing no mercy, the girl took pincer-grips of both his nipples and twisted them, hard. His knees almost buckled but he endured the humiliating torment. Wanda almost felt sorry for him. That Kitty, she was something else! Wanda could never have brought herself to treat a man like that. Now, if a man was to treat *her* that way, that'd be different. Hard to bear, maybe, but different.

Kitty pointed at Chuck's jeans. He shook his head. She said something threatening. He very slowly unbuckled his belt. Kitty, showing impatience, gripped his pants on each side of his lean hips and yanked them down to mid-thigh. Defeated, he skinned them down the rest of the way and kicked out of them in just his boxers. Kitty fisted both of her own hips and made her demands. She pulled his shoulder to face him more directly at the tower, and at Wanda. Crimson-faced, the ranch-hand pushed his underwear down and stood with his hands covering his genitals. The muscles in his thighs were quivering with shame.

Kitty shook her head. She said something forceful. Chuck, as slowly as he dared, moved his hands to link behind his naked bottom. Kitty waggled a finger, telling the lad to revolve, which he did, shuffling. His cock wasn't erect. It stood out at its base but curved down to dangle. Kitty pointed at it and gave a command. Chuck took hold of its shaft between a thumb and his fingers and gave it a long slow stroke, then another. His face was berry-red. He looked on the point of tears. If he'd fantasised about sex with Kitty in the past, which he surely had, this certainly wasn't what he'd imagined it would be like. What was he – nineteen? He'd expect to be the seducer, not the abject sex slave. Wanda had to wonder if he'd be able to perform, sexually, under the circumstances.

His penis answered her question. It had risen to jut up at forty-five degrees, and it looked both thicker and longer.

Kitty nodded to show her approval. She pointed to Wanda's lounger and gave his shoulder a shove. He sank back onto the long seat. Kitty gave more instructions. He raised both hands above his head to grip the top bar of the chaise. Kitty put her hands on his and squeezed, obviously telling him he wasn't allowed to let go of the chaise. She squatted beside him and arranged the poor boy's legs, feet flat on the ground to either side, calves straight up, knees spread wide. With his limbs parted like that, his genitals were totally unprotected, despite the way his thighs twitched from time to time. The urge to cover himself must have been hard to resist, but Kitty had the upper hand. He apparently dared not disobey her.

She perched on the edge of the chaise and leaned over to inspect his cock and balls from close up. His face twitched in a paroxysm of embarrassment. Chuck closed his eyes tightly and bit his lower lip.

Kitty waved to Wanda and pointed at Chuck's now drooping cock. Her eyebrows lifted in a question. Wanda nodded, even though she knew Kitty couldn't see her, giving the girl her permission to continue the sexual torment she was putting her victim through. Wanda changed her grip on the telescope, swapping right hand for left. Her right was needed up under her brief skirt. Why hadn't she thought to bring her vibrator? Oh well, fingers came first, so to speak.

Kitty brushed the backs of her fingers up and down the length of Chuck's shaft. It stiffened instantly. The boy writhed on the spot, seeming desperate to move but terrified of the consequences of disobedience. Wanda's friend took a firm grip on the boy's cock and pumped it, but very, very slowly. A slight adjustment to the telescope's lens brought the lad's glans into sharp focus. It had turned purple and was leaking crystal droplets. How he had to be aching. Wanda could almost envy him. To be humiliated at the same time as being erotically tortured, that had to be a really special feeling.

Chuck's six-pack abdomen rippled. His clenched rump came up off his seat. Kitty spoke to him sharply. He subsided but his persecution continued. Wanda counted. Kitty was taking between three and four lingering seconds on each upstroke and the same down. What an agony of lust the lad had to be suffering!

Kitty's free hand joined the play, toying with the lad's scrotum, jiggling his balls and scratching gently beneath them. The fingers of Wanda's right hand tugged her panties aside.

Chuck was rigid. His biceps bulged. The long muscles in the fronts of his thighs contracted and relaxed, mimicking fucking but not moving him a single inch. Kitty gave Wanda the 'OK' sign and winked. Wanda nodded and found the slippery button of her clitoris with the ball of her thumb. Her index finger curled up inside herself to reach the spongy mass of her G spot. She squeezed. Her clit slipped aside like a wet orange pip but her thumb followed it mercilessly.

Kitty sat herself astride the lounger, lower down, and leaned towards Chuck's erection. Was she relenting? Was she going to give him head as a reward for his servile obedience? It seemed not. She was simply intensifying her torture. Partly turned aside, to give Wanda a better view, she simply gripped the boy's shaft, just below its head, and lapped, once, passing the tip of her tongue across the 'knot' beneath his glans. He jerked. As a preamble to a good strong sucking, Chuck would have enjoyed that, no doubt, but it was the prelude to her simply looking at his manhood for a long count, perhaps a full minute, before repeating the action. He jerked again. His face was screwed up with lust. He was big and strong. Kitty was tiny and weak. He could easily have grabbed her head and thrust his cock halfway down her throat, but he didn't. She had him totally under her control. She'd tamed the lusty beast, utterly, it seemed to Wanda.

By Wanda's count, Kitty lapped the underside of Chuck's cock, flicking its knot at the end of each tongue-stroke, once a minute for a good fifteen minutes. The boy was almost convulsive with cruelly restrained lust. Those of his muscles that weren't straining were twitching. When *was* that naughty girl going to show him some mercy?

The feline in question stood up. What now? She unlaced the bottom of her bikini, tossed it aside and threw one leg over Chuck to bestride his hips, facing Wanda. Kitty lowered herself, perhaps crooning something sexy to him. If it had been Wanda's performance, *she'd* have used her voice to make it worse for him.

Kitty bent to reach down and back between her own wide-spread thighs and took a firm grip on his shaft. She lowered herself. When just an inch separated the flaccid lips of her sex from the engorged dome of Chuck's cock, she paused. The bitch! Down that inch. A little rub, just barely making contact. Another pause. Lower. Lower.

Half of the helmet was lodged between her lips. Slowly, slowly ... A wink at Wanda. Half of his shaft was inside her. Three-quarters. Finally, the entire rigid length. And there she sat, not moving,

Her lips blew a kiss in Wanda's direction. How that little tease was enjoying her power over her helpless victim! Perhaps he begged because Kitty half turned to say something, something sharp and admonishing, no doubt. She lifted herself up, perhaps two inches. Her hips swung left, then right. She did a little bump followed by a long slow rotation, stirring her soft insides with his rigidity. Then down again for another long pause.

Wanda had to give Chuck credit. Most young men, subjected to the treatment that Kitty was subjecting him to, would have climaxed. Perhaps he simply didn't dare.

Wanda would have enjoyed being teased to the point of insanity. Was it the same for men? She'd never treated a man the way Kitty was treating Chuck. Most likely, she couldn't. It just wasn't in her nature. It certainly was in Kitty's, though. Well, even if Wanda couldn't bring herself to treat a man that way, she could still enjoy watching another girl do it.

Kitty lifted again, but all the way off this time. When she'd steered his shaft back into contact, she came down faster. And lifted. And down. Accelerating. So, the lad was finally getting what he craved. That was a relief, and a disappointment.

Past Kitty's body, Wanda could see Chuck's mouth gape open. He had to be bellowing out that ferocious noise that some men make when they near their orgasms. Wanda stroked herself faster, trying to keep up.

Kitty paused, leaned sideways to the little plastic table, grabbed two handfuls of ice cubes, dismounted Chuck's bucking hips and slapped both hands onto him, one icing his balls, the other his shaft.

He froze in place. His cry must have turned from a joyous one to one of anguish, if Wanda could have heard it. He looked like he babbled something, pleading or complaining or just spewing nonsense. His erection wilted. Poor Chuck!

Kitty bestrode him again. She guided his limp length back into position. Smiling at Wanda, the vixen held up both hands. Her right was still full of ice. Her left held her vibrator. She weighed the two, as if deciding on something. The vibrator touched the base of Chuck's shaft. Even with only an inch of it showing, Wanda could see it stiffen. Kitty lifted, trailing her own pussy with the plastic toy. On her descent, she replaced the vibrator with ice. What would that do to a man? He was being fucked by a gorgeous girl but simultaneously getting his cock frozen – or sometimes vibrated on. He'd never know which to expect. The agony!

Well, it looked like being a long morning. Wanda skinned out of the panties she'd been wearing around her knees and settled down in a more comfortable position. How to get the most fun? Perhaps she'd give herself a climax soon, then start over.

She should have brought a snack up into the tower. It looked like all three of them were going to miss lunch.

Chapter Thirteen

The moms came home soon after lunch the next day, both tipsy on shopping. Kitty sent Chuck out to help them bring in their swag. Most of it he heaped onto the eating-room table but Martha and Lucinda scurried straight upstairs with two of their bags each, bags they hadn't let him touch. There were no names on those bags but they were glossy black with lush red lips displayed on each side. Wanda drew her own conclusions as to the nature of the contents.

By the time the moms' loot had been carried up, a horn sounded outside. It was a distinctive chocolate-brown van from UPS. That could only mean one thing – goodies from Henry. This time *everyone* rushed out to see what early Christmas presents Santa Henry had sent them from Europe.

First out of the van was a gigantic wicker hamper from London's Harrods department store. It was intended for Consuela, who cooed with delight and had two of her sons carry it straight to the kitchen. There was also a small parcel for the cook-housekeeper. She ripped it open to find three Hermes scarves, all the same design but in different colours. Her husband, Olaf, got a cubic package, about a foot on each side, which he tucked under his arm and disappeared with. Two of the boys' parcels contained bottles of some sort of exotic booze, and a bottle of cologne each. They seemed happy with their gifts so Wanda assumed that Henry knew what he was doing. Well, of course he did. He *always* did.

Chuck's present was an antique chess set, which didn't seem like much to Wanda but he seemed pleased enough. Another score for Henry – but what had he bought for *her*? That was the important question.

Lucinda squealed and clapped her hands when she opened a box to find a small bottle of perfume. From her reaction, Caro's Poivre had to be something special. Martha, not to be outdone in her reaction to her gift, clutched at her face and sank onto a chair when she unwrapped Clive Christian's Number One.

'Is that a good perfume?' Wanda asked.

Lucinda told her, 'It's one of the most expensive perfumes in the world, as is mine. Henry is being very generous. His business over there must be going very well.'

Kitty's perfume was about a pint of Chanel Number Five. Half an ounce of the actual perfume, not the eau de cologne, was expensive, so that was impressive. Then there were parcels for the three girls who helped Consuela. Annoyingly, they took them away without showing the contents. If they had, it might have given clues as to their past relationships with Wanda's Henry; though it was innocent, of course. Of course.

The next three boxes were all for Wanda. To her frustration, all were marked 'Do Not Open' and were tied with golden cord that was sealed with blobs of green sealing wax that were stamped with Henry's monogram.

'He wants to see you open these,' Wanda's mom consoled her.

'And wear them,' Kitty added. She tapped the boxes one at a time. The labels were Chanel, Givenchy and Fleur of England. 'Suit, gown, lingerie. *Nice* and *naug hty* lingerie.'

Wanda tried to blush and she *was* pleased, but not in an embarrassed kind of way.

The last box was for her and it wasn't marked 'Do Not Open'. It contained a largish bottle of perfume, Clive Christian Imperial Majesty.

Kitty said, 'Wow!'

Both moms clutched at their faces and squealed.

'What?' Wanda asked. 'Expensive?' She held the bottle up, as if it'd bear a mark of quality of some kind.

'Not just "expensive",' Kitty explained. 'See that golden collar around the neck?'

'Yes.'

'It's real gold, solid gold. The diamond set in the collar is a real diamond, three carats, if I remember correctly.'

Lucinda added, 'It's only the most expensive, and exclusive, perfume in the entire world. It's one of a limited edition. Just half a dozen were made.'

'Five,' Martha corrected her.

Lucinda beat that with: 'Plus the customised bottle in the shape of a piano that was made for Sir Elton John. That makes six.'

Kitty said, 'For the price of that bottle of perfume, you could buy a house, Wanda.'

Wanda felt her face, and brain, go totally numb. 'H-how m-much money are we talking about?'

'It's not nice to ask, my dear,' Lucinda told her, 'but, as you have, over two hundred thousand dollars.'

Wanda's trembling fingers set the bottle gently on the table, well away from the edge. She sat down and stared at it. 'What'll I do with it? Where will I keep it?'

Henry's mom told her, 'You'll keep it on your dressing table, of course. When Henry comes home, you will wear it, but use it sparingly please, dear.'

'Oh, I will,' Wanda promised. 'I will.' She turned to Kitty. 'Do me a favour, Kitty? Would you carry it upstairs for me?'

Wanda spent the rest of the day in a state of dizzy euphoria. Love can be overwhelming. It isn't right for a girl to love a man just because he gives her expensive gifts, but, when she already loves the man and *then* he showers her with fabulous presents, her adoration for him can become overwhelming, almost painful. But the bliss! Such incredible bliss!

Wanda must have eaten dinner but she didn't know what Consuela had served or what it tasted like. She must have occupied the time between dinner and bed somehow, but doing what? Most likely she'd talked to people, but who and what about were lost in a mist. All was well, in a wonderful world. For the rest of that day, she didn't even fantasise. She *was* aware that she had a wedding night coming quite soon but what that meant, in terms of physical intimacy, she didn't even try to imagine. It would be perfect, whatever 'perfect' was. That sufficed.

When she woke up the next morning, she was close to sane again, until she saw the bottle on her dressing table. The mist of bliss returned as she stroked the cool glass but it faded again. By the time she got down for breakfast, she was just incredibly happy.

There was a choice of kedgeree or cheese and spinach omelettes. She'd never tried kedgeree so she chose that. It didn't look that appetising but Wanda found that she really enjoyed it. That was going to be her life from then on – trying new things and enjoying them. Pleasures that she couldn't even imagine were in store for her.

As Consuela dished up, Kitty asked her, 'Consuela, can I borrow Chuck for the day? I want to take a ride around the ranch and I'm a bit nervous to go alone.'

Consuela squinted at Kitty, gave Wanda a knowing glance, and nodded.

Kitty looked at Wanda and winked.

When the two riders set off, Wanda peeked down on them from her bedroom window. There was a coil of white cotton cord hanging from the pommel of Chuck's saddle. Who'd be tying who up? It wasn't hard to guess.

Thinking about Kitty and her willing sex slave got Wanda's imagination going again. She hurried to the tower room and moved the telescope over to the window that faced the direction the two had ridden off in. No luck. They'd already disappeared. While she was at the 'scope she panned it around idly. Maybe she'd find that big red barn. Silly! That'd been a fantasy, not real. Hadn't it? Sometimes, in recollection, the difference between fact and fancy was hard to be sure of.

Maybe there'd be something else worth looking at, but not the sunbathing roof. The moms were most likely out there by now, topless, or worse. How about those stables? Two of the ranch-hands were going in, a big burly guy in his forties and a slightly shorter and slimmer, younger man. She hadn't met either, which opened the door for her lurid imagination wide.

She knew she couldn't do what Kitty was doing,

dominate a man, not in real life. Maybe she could do it in a fantasy. First, she'd need a hold over him, like Kitty had over Chuck. Could those handsome two hands have a guilty secret she could use to control them? What if ... Wanda settled back in the big comfy chair, skirt rucked up, ready to play once the warm feeling came over her. Recalling an old and long-lapsed personal ritual, she sang softly to herself. 'Hey diddle, diddle, time for me to fiddle ...'

Now, what would she be wearing? She'd bought a little skirt that she didn't dare wear when her mom was around. It was very low-rise – with a band that came almost six inches lower than her navel, and very short and flirty. With nothing beneath it, she'd be more than ready for some wild sex. Above? All the girls on the ranch seemed to favour gingham shirts, tied between their boobs. That'd work. She had the tits to carry it off. And ballet flats on her feet.

So, she'd follow those two hands into the stable, and ...

Stables are usually icky and stinky but this one had just been cleaned and renovated. There were no horses in it yet. The floor was wooden planks scrubbed almost white. The walls and inside the roof had been white-washed, except for the beams that had been painted black. Overall, it was a much more salubrious place than that gigantic red barn had been. No surprise. The barn had been in a dream, not a fantasy. That's where fantasies beat dreams. You have more control, usually. Even so, fantasies sometimes took strange and unexpected turns. At least, hers did.

Guttural grunts and wet sloppy gulping sounds betrayed the hands' general location. Wanda crept closer, keeping her head well below the level of the stalls' walls. As she got close to the stall the hands were occupying, she dropped to her knees and crawled until she could see in from almost ground level.

They were *magnificent*.

There was a strap-iron manger in the far corner. The bigger of the two men was facing it, holding it in his fists. She'd thought him big and burly but naked he presented a totally different picture. He reminded her of an elder Greek god, such as Zeus. All the statues of the number-one Olympian had shown him as mature and heavy, but all great slabby muscles that were well defined but not ugly, like some of the bodybuilders whose pictures she'd seen. His hips were relatively lean, as was his bum, that slowly clenched and relaxed in a steady, tightly controlled rhythm. Those beautiful smooth muscles would be as hard to the touch as his biceps, she was sure.

His lover was crouched down before him. Wanda couldn't see the younger man's face but his body could have posed for Michelangelo's David, or a statue of Adonis. Slighter and less muscled than the older man, he was, nevertheless, *gorgeous*. The only things about what

117

she could see of him that didn't fit his being a statue of a Greek god were his two dangling, swaying balls, and the curved column of a beautiful erection that stood high enough to bounce against his navel.

Adonis was gripping Zeus' thighs, just above his knees. As Wanda watched, the lad ran his palms up the insides of the man's legs, to his bum. His hands prized those sculptured cheeks apart and wormed a finger high up between them. With that intimate control, he pulled Zeus closer, driving the man's cock into his own mouth, then tugged him away, and back ...

Adonis had assumed control over the way Zeus fucked his mouth. That contradicted Wanda's first impression of the big one dominating the small one. Perhaps they were sexual equals, each giving what the other needed and taking what he wanted for himself, in perfect harmony? That was a nice thought. No 'do as you would be done by' but 'do unto others as they would like to be done to'. That was utopian. Would it be like that with her and Henry? But what, exactly, was it that she wanted him to do to her?

Adonis was rising up between Zeus' outstretched arms. Wanda flinched back, but unnecessarily. The smaller man had his back, and bum, turned towards the larger. He thrust that bum backwards. Zeus reached down between their bodies. His hips swayed as he positioned himself. He thrust. Adonis gasped, in pleasure, not pain. Both men writhed, point and counterpoint, wallowing deliciously in their respective roles, impaled and impaler. Ying and yang. It seemed a shame to interrupt them but she too had needs. It was *her* fantasy, after all.

Wanda stood tall and walked boldly into the stall. 'What do you think Mr Henry would say if he knew what two men got up to during their working days?'

Zeus, not the least fazed, still grinding against his lover's buttocks, turned his head. 'The ranch is a seven-days-a-week operation, Miss. It happens that this is our weekend – our time off. As for what we do, Mr Henry knows that we are lovers. He had no problem with that.' The big man grinned and turned towards Wanda, flipping his erection out of Adonis and displaying it to her admiring gaze. '*My* question is, what would Mr Henry think if he knew that his fiancée spied on his hands in their most intimate moments, and walked around dressed like *this*?' He reached out and flipped Wanda's tiny skirt up a couple of inches, exposing her naked sex for a brief moment. 'And this?' He tugged on the bow that secured her shirt, releasing it to dangle to each side of her bare breasts.

Wanda managed, 'Um?'

Adonis turned. 'We aren't gay,' he told Wanda. 'We're bisexual. There's no reason we shouldn't all be good friends, we three. What's the expression these days? "Friends with privileges? Fuck buddies?"'

119

'I ...'

Zeus took her wrist and guided Wanda's hand to his fever-hot cock – the cock that had just emerged from Adonis' bum. 'Did you ever play with two men at once before, Wanda?'

Well, she had, but only in fantasy, so it really didn't count, so she shook her head. Then again, *this* was a fantasy, also, so perhaps she wasn't being entirely honest.

'I'd only do something like that if I was forced to,' she hinted.

'That could be arranged,' Adonis said.

Zeus nodded, and stroked himself with Wanda's hand. Damn, but he was big, both ways, length and girth. She wrapped her fingers around it but couldn't make her thumb touch their tips by over an inch. *Formidable!* She shivered in anticipation. A girl can't help but compare, can she? Adonis' cock was just as long as Zeus', but slimmer. Taking two men at once pretty well meant being made into a sandwich. That would ...

Adonis interrupted her thought with: 'If you were bound, you'd have no choice, would you, Wanda.' It wasn't a question.

She shook her head.

Adonis reached out, over the stall's wall, and fished back a tangle of leather straps. They had to be horse tack. Thank goodness, she couldn't see a bridle and bit among them. She'd have to know a man really well before

120

she'd play at being a pony for him. That'd never been among her fantasies, though now she'd thought of it ...

Zeus pulled her shirt off her shoulders. Adonis slid her skirt down to her feet. The two men took her arms. With a few deft movements, they had her wrists secured in leather bands and stretched out to both sides, where the leather was secured over black iron hooks that were set in the walls' uprights.

She was helpless. Struggling would be useless. If she screamed, no one would hear her. Wanda was totally at the mercy of two powerful and horny men. She was nothing but a toy for them to use however they wished, no matter how demeaning.

How *delicious*!

Adonis, standing behind her, ran his palms down from her neck, caressing her sides and hips. Zeus, in front of her, held her throat firmly but gently in one hand while the other slid down between her trembling breasts, cupped them, jiggled them, and smoothed over her nipples so delicately it almost tickled. His hand drifted lower, following the curve of her belly to her pubic mound, which it cupped and compressed in a slow steady rhythm. To her shame, Wanda felt herself oozing into Zeus' palm.

'Aphrodite in bondage,' he whispered. 'Give me your ambrosia.' His lips nibbled into the crook of her neck. 'Goddess and whore. Empress of all the harlots. How sweet you are. Let me taste you.' His mouth slid across her cheek. Wanda couldn't help but turn her face towards his kiss. His tongue was strong, very masculine, very demanding.

Behind her, Adonis was working his way down her back, lapping at her spine, down and down, past her waist, down to her tailbone, which he slavered with wet kisses and nibbled on with tiny delicate bites.

Wanda felt Adonis' open hand cover her bottom. No – both hands, one on each cheek. They moved apart, spreading her cheeks. He nuzzled into her crease. His tongue wiggled. Oh yes! She could tell what it was that he intended to do to her and it was something very naughty. She ought to protest but Zeus' tongue in her mouth wouldn't allow that. In any case, what Adonis was about to do to her was ...

Oh fuck! That was *so* good. The young man's tongue was very strong, and incredibly long. He'd actually managed to force it *into* her. He was tongue-fucking her bum! Wanda spread her legs and hollowed her back, pushing back at him, encouraging the deepest penetration he could manage. It felt very wet, as if he was deliberately making spit.

As a lubricant?

Adonis stood erect. The prod that Wanda felt between her buttocks confirmed her suspicion. She concentrated on relaxing the tight ring of muscle that was feeling pressure that started as subtle but soon became intense, and ... Her flesh surrendered and stretched. This had to be the best part of being taken, she thought, the moment when her body's resistance was overcome and the rigid invader was welcomed. Deeply. So deeply. A probe of very solid flesh dilated her. It was obscene – what Adonis was doing to her. It was even more obscene that she was enjoying every depraved moment. She was so *bad*. She *deserved* to be abused and violated. Debauchery came naturally to her, it seemed. Wanda was thoroughly ashamed of herself and enjoyed that emotion, as well.

Would Henry shame her the way she needed?

Best not to think about that. Not in the middle of a decadent fantasy. It was too serious a question.

Zeus deserted her mouth. His lips trailed down her neck, further, to her breast. He suckled, soft then hard, before moving lower. His tongue slithered down her lower belly, leaving a trail of tickling saliva. The big man's mouth opened wide, covering her entire pubic mound. His strong white teeth threatened her, playfully, before his tongue lapped out between her pussy's lips and slavered over her clit.

Adonis' thrusts from behind impelled Wanda's hips forward so that she was compelled to grind at Zeus' mouth. She spread her thighs further apart and humped at the big man's tongue, each movement tightening her behind on Adonis' hardness. She was the sex slave, in leather bondage, but her eager participation made her an equal partner in their debauchery.

'You bitch!' Adonis complimented her.

'Bite me!' she replied.

He obeyed by hunching over to nip at her nape.

Much as she was enjoying the things that Zeus' mouth was doing to her, this fantasy had a logical direction to follow. She told Zeus, 'Now fuck me!'

He looked up with a grin. 'Silly girl! What makes you think you can call the shots here? I'll fuck you, all right, but when I'm good and ready.' He stood, dwarfing her.

From that close, his bulk was intimidating. His nipples were at the level of her eyes. She could feel his erection's head tap on her skin, just inches below her breasts. If it'd been inside her, he'd have lifted her on that fleshy staff, leaving her legs dangling. Was she ready for that?

His great fist took hold of Wanda's hair, pulling at its roots. He took half a step backwards and tugged, forcing her to double over at her waist. That pushed her harder back at Adonis and drove the young man even higher up inside her. Zeus swayed, wagging his cock so that it slapped against her cheek. Instinctively, Wanda opened wide. At full stretch, her lips managed to encompass its head. Adonis thrust hard, driving Wanda forward and Zeus deeper into her mouth. Zeus pushed back, impaling her bottom harder on Adonis. Together, they rocked her.

It was almost as if she was impaled on a spit of flesh that went right through her. Her stretched arms ached at her shoulders but she couldn't do anything to ease the strain. She'd been reduced to nothing but a sex toy, rocking to and fro, pleasing two men who cared nothing for her apart for her use as an *object*.

Adonis gripped her hips tightly enough that his fingers would leave bruises. Zeus mangled her left breast with the hand that wasn't gripping her head. She had no control, none. They didn't care if she enjoyed their torment of her weak little body. If she climaxed, it'd mean nothing to them. They did what they did, for their pleasure, not for hers. Wanda was sure that Adonis cared about Zeus' fun, and that concern was reciprocated, but she? She was *nothing* to them.

There was a certain freedom in that.

Wanda swayed. The leather straps creaked. The men, from time to time, grunted.

Eventually, Adonis said, 'Pause?'

Both men stilled.

Zeus replied, 'Want to beat her next?'

'No. You know what I want. We haven't done it since the Christmas party. It was good, remember?'

'The girl screamed, as I recall.'

'From joy.'

'You think this one will?'

'Only one way to find out.'

'Want to switch, then?' Zeus asked.

'She's very tight back here. She's not been taken very often, by the feel of her.'

'I like that! Very well, let's swap places.'

Wanda panted, 'What?'

'You'll soon see,' Adonis told her. 'It'll be good, I promise.'

Wasn't that nice of him!

The men ducked under Wanda's arms, changing places.

'You'd better go first,' Adonis told Zeus. 'But be careful of your back.'

'I will,' the big man said. His hands took hold of Wanda's hips. He heaved her up.

She felt his staff nudge her right cheek, then her left. It slid between her legs to protrude in front of her, like she'd grown a penis.

'Let me help,' Adonis said. He crouched down and took hold of his lover's shaft in one hand while the fingers of his other parted Wanda's cheeks.

Zeus pushed forward.

'That's it,' Wanda told them, encouragingly. 'Right there.'

Zeus thrust. Thank goodness she'd already been opened up by Adonis; otherwise it would have been unbearable. Zeus slid into her, stretching her much wider than his smaller companion had done. It was hard to take, in the best possible way. Wanda bit her lip and endured, and endured, and it went higher and deeper until, at long last, she felt the short curly hairs on his pubes grind against her tailbone.

Then he lifted her on it.

Hell! Somehow he'd managed to go even further into her than Adonis had. She dangled there, feet off the floor, impaled. It was beyond anything a normal girl could possibly imagine. Luckily, Wanda wasn't a normal girl. She was some sort of sex addict, with an overactive imagination.

It was the smaller man's turn. He introduced himself to her neglected pussy, and pushed. It was like she was a virgin again. With her behind so full, her vagina had been squashed flat. Adonis forced it to open again, inch by slow inch.

'Can you feel that?' he asked Zeus.

'Oh yes. How about this?' The big man jiggled Wanda.

Inside her, the shaft rubbed against the head of the smaller man's erection. They were fucking each other, through her! What did that make her?

They alternated, Zeus sliding in as Adonis slid out, caressing each other through the thin slippery membrane that divided Wanda's bum from her sex. Zeus nibbled on her neck. Adonis devoured her mouth. Wanda, suspended between the men, surrendered to bliss. Her mind blanked but the warmth inside her grew. She was a marionette, but with sweet sensations. Her clit tingled. There was pressure building. She screamed, 'Yes!'

Adonis said, 'I told you so.'

Zeus asked, 'Now?'

'Yeah, now!'

Both men jerked, almost convulsed. Wanda felt their hot foam flood up into her, front and back, and juddered into her second and third orgasms.

And, in the tower room, her phone chimed out the first bars of the overture to *Phantom of the Opera*.

Chapter Fourteen

Wanda said, 'Hello?'

It was Kitty. 'Sorry to have neglected you, Wanda. Are you finding ways to amuse yourself?'

'No problem, Kitty-cat. I've just been idling away, thinking, mostly.'

'Thinking sexy thoughts?'

'Maybe,' Wanda admitted. 'How's your "ride" with Chuck going for you?'

'Oh, about as you'd expect.'

'That naughty, huh?'

'I'd have brought you along,' Kitty said, 'but you'd have felt uncomfortable about joining in, right?'

'You know me. Lookee, lookee, no touchee.'

'How about listening? Would you like me to tell you what we're up to – and doing right now?'

'Is it shocking?'

'Could be; for some.'

'Hold on a minute, then, and I'll be all ears.'

Wanda put her eye to the 'scope, just to check. The younger man was holding the stable door open for the older one, who was pushing a wheelbarrow full of manure. So much for Wanda's pristine stable!

Her panties were uncomfortably saturated from her fantasy. She slipped them down and off before resuming her comfy position in the chair. She switched the phone to her left hand and rested her right up her skirt, cupping her sex. 'I'm ready now,' she told Kitty. 'Give me all the nasty details. Don't miss a single thing.'

Kitty's voice took on a sing-song kindergarten-teacher lilt. 'Are you sitting comfortably, Wanda?'

'Yes.'

'Then I'll begin.' She cleared her throat. 'Chuck and I set off towards the new growth of young trees that Henry planted a few years back. There are no trails leading there, yet, and it's in a little valley, so it's pretty much private.'

Wanda interrupted. 'Is it anywhere near that pretty pond with the enormous weeping willow?'

'Nowhere even close.'

That was a relief. Wanda planned to take Henry back there someday to finish what he'd started. Until then, she considered the shady tree 'theirs'.

Kitty continued. 'I let Chuck know that I was looking for a special kind of place but not what it was, to keep him in suspense. Subbies like that.'

'Subbies?'

'Sexually submissive people, of both sexes. It gets their adrenaline going.'

Wanda made a mental note that it seemed she wasn't alone in that. Being made to wait for punishment had always got her motor revving. At high school, she'd done a few mildly naughty things just to get sent to the principal's office. She'd fantasised while she waited that her punishment would be corporal, perhaps ten strokes of the cane on her bare bottom. It never was, though. Life can be disappointing sometimes.

Kitty continued. 'The young trees had been planted at random, but not too close together, so it took me a while to find four that suited my plans. They were pretty sturdy and growing at the four corners of a square that was about seven feet to a side. I ordered Chuck to strip naked and lie in the middle of the square, spread-eagle. Then I used the cord we'd brought to tie his wrists and ankles to the trees.' Kitty paused.

'And then?' Wanda prompted.

'I went for a little walk. Just fifteen minutes or so. More suspense for him, you see. He found that agonising, didn't you, sweetie?'

Wanda heard Chuck's muffled 'Yes' in the background. He was still *there*! How humiliating it had to be for him to have to listen to Kitty talking about how she'd dominated him.

Kitty said, 'We'd brought a picnic lunch. When I got back I took my top off and ate it, allowing him the odd bite now and then, but of food, not of me, even though he begged. Once we'd eaten, I teased him some more by writing messages on his face and chest with my nipples. I threaten to punish him if he couldn't tell me what I'd written. The poor boy failed miserably, of course, because I only wrote nonsense. For a punishment, I teased his privates with blades of grass, then stuck some stiff stems up his bum.'

'Inside?'

'Where else? That was so much fun that I took an old silk scarf that I just happened to have with me, tied knots in it every few inches, buttered it the whole length and then pushed the knots into his bum, one at a time, very slowly. They're still there, Wanda.'

'Still there? You haven't let him pull them out?'

'He's tied to four trees, remember.'

'Still!'

'Still. I'm not done with my Chuck, not yet. I thought you'd like to be in on the end.'

'So he's still tied up, or down, whatever?'

'Oh yes.'

'He's very quiet,' Wanda observed.

'He doesn't have much choice. I'm sitting on his face.'

'What?'

'I'm sitting on his face. My naked pussy is over his mouth. His nose is between the cheeks of my bum. Don't

132

worry. When I think he's distressed, I ease up and let him breathe.'

'That's very kind of you, Kitty.'

'Yes, it is, isn't it? So, I've got my phone in my left hand and I'm using my right to give his cock a slap from time to time, to keep it nice and stiff.' Kitty's voice became stern. 'Lick, damn you, Chuck. Lick harder!' To Wanda, in her softer voice, she said, 'I'm laying the phone down, dear. You should still be able to hear me OK. I need both hands now. Just a sec.'

From a slight distance but still perfectly audible, Kitty continued, 'I'm buttering my hand, Wanda, and I have to lean forward. There. I've got hold of the end of my scarf with one hand and I'm stroking him with the other one, the buttery one. Just call me "butter fingers".'

Wanda chuckled.

'He can breathe a bit easier now, but that doesn't mean he can stop licking.'

Chuck said something but Wanda couldn't make the words out.

Kitty said, 'I don't care if your tongue aches, Chuck. You just get it back on my clit and keep on licking.' To Wanda, she said, 'I'm stroking him slowly, up and down, and pulling just a little bit on the scarf, not enough to pull it out, just enough that he can feel the pressure – from inside!' Kitty panted. 'That's right, Chuck, right there, but harder and faster.'

Wanda rolled her own clit between her thumb and finger. 'Are you going to let him come?' she asked.

'I think so. I'm getting close, myself. I think this dominating thing is *my* thing, if you know what I mean.'

'I can understand that,' Wanda said, though she couldn't. It seemed unnatural, somehow, for the woman to be in charge. Though, if the woman was dominating another woman, that didn't seem quite so strange. She could see enjoying that, if she was the submissive one.

'He's getting really tense,' Kitty said in a rushed, breathless voice. 'I think he's close. Are you close, Chuck?'

His answer was an anguished garbled cry.

'Seems he is. I'm going to pump harder and faster, Wanda. He's going to give me a nice big come, aren't you, Chuck. You're going to make a fountain for me, aren't you? Show me how much come you can make, there's a good boy. Yes, I can feel it coming. Here it comes! And I pull the first knot out of your bum, and the second, and you're squirting right up into the air. More, Chuck. Show me what you've got. Yes! Yes! Yes! And me too! I'm there!'

There was a moment's silence, then Kitty sighed. 'That was very nice. Good boy, Chuck. Don't worry, I brought wet-wipes. Once I release you, you can clean us both up.' To Wanda, she said, 'Was it good for you, Wanda, dear?'

'Very interesting,' Wanda allowed.

'Did you climax?'

'Of course,' Wanda lied. 'See you later. Bye.' She clicked off. Damn. If the call had lasted just a few more minutes, she'd have got there. Of course, she'd already got off on her stable fantasy. Anyway, all she had to do now was keep diddling herself and come up with another erotic scene to imagine. Let's see …

Chapter Fifteen

Just after supper, Olaf came in and announced, 'He's on his way. About ten minutes.'

Wanda gathered that Olaf was in charge of radio communications with Henry's plane. If she'd known earlier, she could have pestered him into putting her in touch with her fiancé.

Ten minutes!

She tore upstairs, stripped, retouched her face, quickly but subtly so as not to offend her mom, pulled on panties, hose and her 'little black dress'. She chose three-inch heels. Those would make her mom sniff but not forbid. Wanda was halfway out of her bedroom door before she remembered to dash back to her dressing table to dab her outrageously expensive perfume onto her temples and wrists.

She got back downstairs just as Henry came in through the front door. His chin was shadowed, as were his eyes. There was less spring in his stride. She got a hug, during which he inhaled strongly, and a peck on her lips.

'I like the perfume,' he said. 'Do you?'

'Love it.' She moved in for a better kiss but the moms and Kitty all arrived at once for their hugs and to give air-kisses, forcing Wanda to back off. Bitches!

Henry said, 'Sorry, but it's been hectic and I've been in the air for over twenty hours today – today and yesterday. I'm going up to bed. I'll say hello properly tomorrow morning. We leave at ten.'

From the background, Consuela demanded, 'Food!'

'I snacked as I flew. Make me a special breakfast, please?'

'Humph!'

He said, 'Night!' and was gone, leaving Wanda feeling cold and empty.

And angry. He was her fiancé, dammit! When was he going to start treating her like his bride-to-be? Was this what her life with him was going to be like? 'Hello goodbye'? A peck and a hug and off to sleep? If that was how it would be, she'd take a lover. No, two lovers. Maybe three? She'd give Kitty what she'd been begging for. Maybe she'd include Chuck. Her silly old fantasies? They were tame compared to what she'd get up to if Henry didn't start treating her like a real, live, horny, woman.

Damn!

Wanda showered and tried to get herself off under the beating hot water but the feeling just wouldn't come. In

137

just her bathrobe, she crept downstairs, where it was all dark by then, and found a bottle of vodka to take back up to bed with her. She fell asleep before she'd solved the mystery of getting the top off.

The special breakfast that Consuela made for Henry was referred to as 'full British'. There were eggs and back bacon and some organ meats and lamb chops, fried tomatoes and Portobello mushrooms, plus home fries. It was accompanied by toast and ginger marmalade. Henry ate as if he was famished, to Consuela's delight. Wanda took one egg, two small pieces of bacon and half a slice of toast. She'd been eating too much. Anyway, if she ate very little while Henry devoured his food like a wolf, perhaps it'd make him feel guilty.

If he noticed.

Wanda lingered over getting ready. She'd chosen stretchy jeans that fit her legs, and bum, like pantyhose. Over it, she wore a big floppy shirt to cover up how low-rise the jeans were. It also hid her lack of the bra she didn't need. She waited at the window until the luggage was loaded and everyone else got aboard. It was time for take-off. She still waited. At last, Olaf called up the stairs, 'They're all waiting for you, Miss Wanda!'

Good. Now, no matter what, her mom couldn't send her back to change her clothes.

She sauntered over to the landing strip, rolling her hips. Her mom and Lucinda would be in the passenger cabin, being served drinks by 'stew' Kitty. They wouldn't be looking out but Henry might be.

Once aboard, she headed straight for the pilot's cabin, scruffing her shirt up high and knotting it as she went. Here, Mr Henry, Sir, take a look at *this* svelte midriff, if you will. Want some of this? Better get it while it's still hot!

Wanda had the small satisfaction of seeing Henry's eyes widen when she sank into the navigator's seat. Then he was talking pilot-talk into his mic and the plane started rolling.

When they were in the air, he reached over and put his hand on her knee. Damn! She should have worn a skirt or a dress. A short one. And gone 'commando'.

'Wanda,' he said, 'it's been hard on you, me being away on business so much.'

She nodded.

'One thing I've been doing that might interest you is arranging our honeymoon.'

She laid her hand over his and waited. Whatever he had to say, it had better be good. Honeymoon arrangements should be by mutual agreement, the arrogant bastard!

'I've booked us the honeymoon suite at the Palace, for our first night, then a cruise to Tahiti and made us reservations at an excellent hotel there.'

Oh? A cruise ship to Tahiti was hard to resent.

'Then on to Rio. You'll love Rio. You dance, of course?'

Her fiancé didn't know even that much about her? 'Of course,' she said.

'Latin American?'

'Like the mambo and cha-cha?'

'I was thinking more along the lines of the tango and lambada.'

'Oh? Well, no, then.'

'That's OK. You'll need the right clothes, of course, and to take dancing lessons. I'll make arrangements.'

'The right clothes? I have dresses for dancing.'

'I'm sure that you have but in Rio the way the women dress to dance is quite special. You'll see. It'll please me to outfit you appropriately so leave that to me. Anyway, from Rio, to Rome and Paris, for shopping, then to London, where I'll introduce you to some people and we can do all the touristy things, The Tower, The Eye, and so on. Some of the stately homes, maybe.'

'Isn't that a lot of travelling to pack into one honeymoon?'

'I don't think so.' He squeezed her thigh and chuckled. 'Why do you think I've been so busy, clearing my slate, making free time? The way I have it planned, and booked, our honeymoon will take three full months and two more days. That should give us ample time to really get to know each other.'

He'd been working himself ragged to give them time for a three-month honeymoon? And she'd resented it?

Oh, Henry! Maybe he could put the plane on autopilot so she could show her appreciation? It'd be a bit cramped for sex in here, but the least she could do would be to give him a nice loving blow job. Would that shock him?

'Does your plane have autopilot?' she asked, working up to her offer.

'Yes, Wanda, it does, but this little hop doesn't take long enough to make it worthwhile. We're coming into our descent already.'

Fuck! Too late. He wouldn't know it but she'd give him a rain cheque on the oral sex. And she'd never doubt him again, ever!

Chapter Sixteen

Dr Sullivan turned a page of Wanda's notes and asked, 'This one, with Kitty and Chuck in the forest, was that real or a fantasy?'

'I was just there by phone, but I *think* it was real.'

'So you don't remember getting any fantasy phone calls? I mean calls that you just imagined getting?'

'I don't think so. It's hard to be absolutely sure. None from aliens from outer space, though, if that's the kind of thing you mean. I've never fantasised an alien abduction.'

'I see.' He turned another page. 'And did you perform oral sex on your fiancé while he was flying his plane?'

'No, that was a wish, not a fantasy and not for real.'

'The barn thing was definitely a fantasy?'

'Oh yes, for sure. I'd never ... Not in real life. That's OK, isn't it, Doctor?'

'In a fantasy, anything and everything is "OK". I'm not here to judge your love life, anyway. Your concern, and mine, is for you to be able to tell reality from imagination, and for you to gain more control over your – er – daydreams. "Control" doesn't mean stop having them, if you need them, or just enjoy them. It just means your being able to function fully in the real world.'

'Do you get many patients with my sort of problem, Doctor?' Wanda asked.

'I can't discuss my other patients. You know that.'

'Not in general terms?'

'No.'

'It'd help me to know I wasn't alone.'

'Everyone fantasises, Wanda. It's just a matter of how often and what about.'

Wanda leaned forward in her chair. 'Are my fantasies *hotter* than most other people's, Doctor?'

He drew back. 'They're yours. That's what's important. Oh, look at the time. Next week, same time?'

'Of course, Doctor.' Had she embarrassed the poor man? Was it bad of her to find that funny? A girl can't help but be proud of having the sexiest fantasies, can she? Or should she be ashamed of it? She'd ask him next week. Maybe by then she'd have had one that was even wilder than her one set in the stable, the one with Zeus and Adonis.

On the subway, Wanda concentrated on doing her Kegels. That always turned her attention inwards, so it helped prevent her from being lured into fantasy-land by any of the other passengers. It worked but by the time she got home she was feeling quite needy, which was the usual side effect of the exercise.

Her mom wanted to talk about the guest list for the wedding.

Wanda said, 'That sounds like fun. I'll just take a quick shower and we'll do that.'

'What's your password? I'll get started.'

That'd give Wanda more time in the shower so she said, 'Bar C 123,' before she realised that perhaps it wasn't a good idea for her mom to have access to her computer files. She quickly added, 'Here, I'll bring it up for you.' She took the laptop, logged in and brought the wedding list file up. 'There you go, Mom!' Wanda made a mental note to change her password as soon as possible.

In her bedroom, she'd just dropped her skirt when the phone rang.

Kitty said, 'You've got mail!'

'Hi, Kitty. What do you mean?'

'Parcels, here, at my place, for you, care of me. Lots of them.'

'Why would they come to you and not directly here?'

'At a wild guess and seeing that they're from Henry, I'd say they contain things that he doesn't think you'd like your mom to see.'

'Oh! Are they to be opened later, or now?'

'They don't say. Want me to open them for you?'

'Don't you dare! Can I come over right now?'

'I've already opened the wine. Why don't we have a sleepover? Want to ask your mom?'

'*Tell* her, you mean.'

'If you say so. I know you don't like to drive but I'm only fifteen minutes from where you are. Get a cab. Henry can afford it. We could send out for pizza or Chinese, make each other's face up, do each other's nails, all sorts of girly-girly stuff. Wouldn't that be fun?'

'No funny stuff?'

'I've got some porn movies we can share, but I know your rules – lookee, lookee, no touchee. That's fine by me, unless you change your mind. I won't pressure you, honest.'

'Give me half an hour.'

'Can't wait. Bye!'

Wanda pulled her skirt back up, grabbed a few things from the bathroom, called a cab and went to the dining room, where her mom was. She announced, 'I'm off to Kitty's. I'll need this.' She picked up her laptop. 'Sorry, Mom. We'll get to the guest list tomorrow, when I get back. Promise.' She rushed out before her mom had a chance to digest the implications of 'Tomorrow, when I get back.'

Kitty's apartment was on the thirtieth floor of a luxury high-rise. Obviously, the girl didn't lack for funds, even if she did seem to be unemployed. When she opened the door, Wanda's friend was wearing a pink silk nightshirt that had buttons and buttonholes from neck to hem. One button was done up. Wanda looked Kitty up and down. She raised an eyebrow.

'Sleepover, right?' Kitty said. 'Come on in. It's draughty out here.'

Wanda followed Kitty's swaying hips. 'That's how you dress at two in the afternoon?'

'Be prepared, right?'

'Prepared for what?'

Kitty turned and shrugged, sliding her shirt off one delectable shoulder. 'Whatever.' She shrugged again, fully exposing her left breast.

'You're a bitch,' Wanda said. 'You said "no pressure".'

'True. Pressure is "pushing". I won't do that. All I'll do is tempt you into making the first move, then all bets are off. I look on you as a challenge, dearest Wanda. I won't rest until I've …'

'Seduced me? Does Henry know what you're like?'

'Could be. He's pretty observant. I'd hate to assume that he misses anything.'

'Yet he still throws me in your path?'

'Perhaps he hopes I'll succeed?'

'Or maybe he's testing me.'

'Hoping for what result? That you'll resist or that you will succumb to my evil wiles?'

That was a thought. Most men thought about three-somes. What if Henry's secret fantasy was making love to her and Kitty together? How did she feel about that?

146

No, couldn't be. That sort of thing came long after the honeymoon was well and truly over. She'd make sure that it never was over, not ever.

She told Kitty, 'He's your cousin, remember? If he wanted to set me up with another girl for a ménage, it'd be someone else, not you.'

Kitty pulled a sour face. 'Could be that you're right. So, how about all those pretty parcels, or did you want to get comfortable first?'

'I'm comfy enough. Show me to the goodies!'

Kitty's dining table was piled high with colourful packages, all addressed to Wanda, care of Kitty.

Wanda said, 'Wow! Where do I start?'

'Smallest to biggest?'

'Sounds like a plan. Smallest is usually best, when it comes to pressies.'

Kitty fished out a parcel that was about twice the size of a cigar box. 'Try this one, then.'

Wanda ripped the paper off and opened the cardboard box. There was tissue to discard, exposing stockings. 'Stockings?' she said, a bit disappointed.

Kitty lifted up the top pair. 'Signs of things to come. Look at this, Wanda. Black, with lovely lacey tops, another pair in black, with seams up the backs. Blue. Green. Purple. Red. Gold and silver, fishnet and very long ... It's a veritable cornucopia of leg-adornments. Think about what it means.'

'What?'

'One, he likes your legs, a lot. Two, I'm betting that there's a pair for each outfit he's bought for you. You said he was buying you club wear, for Latin dancing? That's what must be in the other boxes, what, maybe a dozen different sexy outfits?'

'How do you know they're all sexy?'

'Fishnet stockings, under something dowdy? Glittery gold hose, under an old-lady-style frock? Could you imagine that?'

Wanda brightened. 'I guess not. OK, what's the next size up?'

Kitty selected a box that was covered in matte-black fabric and tied with golden cords. 'This one has the fanciest wrappings. Just a sec.' She returned with scissors. 'Use these.'

Wanda was careful not to puncture the cloth, just in case – of what, she wasn't sure. Inside was a full dress in black knit jersey. 'It looks far too small.'

'It's stretchy. Try it on and see.'

'Now?'

'You're going to open all these fabulous gifts without trying anything on? What are you made of, stone?'

'You're right. Do you have a robe I could borrow?'

Kitty looked her friend up and down with one eyebrow raised. '*Do* I?'

'Something that isn't like that shirt you are deliberately

falling out of please. Something more modest.' Damn! She'd used her mom's watchword. 'modest'.

'Spoilsport!'

'You're right, again, Kitty.' Mainly to counteract her use of the word 'modest', Wanda dropped her skirt and discarded her blouse. That left her bare-breasted but at least she still had her bikini panties on.

'You can't wear anything at all under that dress,' Kitty told her. 'Nothing. Nada. Zip.'

Wanda held the dress up to inspect it. Without her body in it, it looked about half her size. 'Maybe you're right. Turn around, then.'

'Wanda, we've seen everything there is to see of each other, remember? Sunbathing? The roof? Watching each other "at play".'

'That was different, somehow. Here, alone with you in your apartment, it seems more … intimate. Be a doll and just turn, please?'

Kitty pulled a sour face but she turned her back to Wanda. Wanda skinned out of her panties and pulled the dress over her head. So far, so good, but she had to pinch and tug, pinch and tug, to work it down over her body. The neck was a wide deep 'V', so popping her head out of the top was no problem, even if the long sleeves were. When Wanda emerged enough to be able to see, Kitty was looking straight at her.

'Yummy!'

'You said you wouldn't watch me put it on!'

'You only asked me to turn around, so I did. Around and around. It just happened I ended up facing you, dearest Wanda.'

'Bitch!'

'Yes I am, thanks. That's what you love about me, Wanda.'

'What do you think of this dress?'

'I've got mirror doors on my bedroom closets. Come see for yourself.' She began gathering Wanda's presents up into her arms.

'What are you doing?'

'Saving time. You want to change out here and then go into my bedroom every time, or shall we just move the entire show into the other room and be done with it?'

'Makes sense,' Wanda allowed. Her eyes narrowed. 'This isn't just your way to lure me into your bedroom, is it?'

'I wouldn't need a bed to do you on, Wanda. There's lots of furniture in here, and then there's always the floor. Which would you prefer, bent over a footstool or spread along the couch, for starters?'

'You're bad.'

'Badder than you could possibly dream.'

'I guess I'll never know about that.'

'Never say never, right?'

They carried all the parcels into Kitty's bedroom, which

had to be by far the largest room in the apartment, Wanda guessed. It had lots of mirrors, a king-sized bed, two chaises, and was decorated in pink and scarlet, with oversized animal-print pillows, much like Wanda imagined a bordello bedroom would be like.

'No mirror in the ceiling over your bed?' she joked.

'I'll have one put up, if you like.'

'I'll make do with a vertical reflection, thanks.'

'So, what do you think of your vertical reflection?'

Wanda studied herself in the mirror. The jersey clung like a second skin, even to indenting into her navel and silhouetting her nipples. The scoop of the neckline gave her a deep cleavage and the ankle-length skirt was slit to where the tops of her stocking would have been, were she wearing them.

'He got your measurements exactly right,' Kitty commented.

'From that Mr Pink, I guess. I thought he took a lot of unnecessary measurements when he was fitting me for my riding habit.'

'So, what do you think?'

'Dare I wear it in public?'

'I don't think that Henry will give you any choice. That's not his way, as I'm sure you've discovered. Anyway, it's for Latin dancing, in Rio, right? I've been there, done that. By Rio lambada standards, what you have on is relatively modest.'

'I don't like that word.'

'What word?'

'Modest.'

'OK, I won't use it then. Conservative?'

'I think I'm learning about a whole new side of Henry,' Wanda said.

'You like the new side that you're seeing?'

'Oh yes, very much. Kitty, this might sound gushy and teenager-ish, but the more I learn about Henry, the more I love him.'

'Aw! That's lovely. I hope you go on finding many more reasons to love him, for the rest of your life.'

Wanda couldn't help but hug Kitty for that, but the bitch took advantage to grope her bum and grind pubes, so she pulled away.

'You started it that time,' Kitty said.

'And now I'm finishing it. What's next?'

'Shall I help you off with that?'

'No thanks. Next?'

'When you wear that dress for real, add those stockings with the seams and the highest heels you can dance in. You'll kill!'

'Thanks for the tip. How about this one?' Wanda picked up a gold-wrapped parcel and ripped the paper off. 'More hosiery?' She pulled the garment out of the box. No, not stockings, it's ...' Wanda held it up in front of herself. 'Can it be a dress?'

Kitty clapped and jumped up and down, letting her loose shirt flap up higher than her navel. 'Try it on! Try it on!'

Throwing all caution, and damned modesty, to the winds, Wanda peeled herself out of the black jersey dress. She shot a hip at Kitty. 'Suffer, Kitty-cat. Watch me all you like. Lookee, lookee, no touchee, remember. On your own head be it.'

'Such sweet suffering!' Kitty put a thoughtful fingertip to her dimpled chin and cocked her head. 'Is that from Shakespeare or did I just make it up?'

'A bit of each, I think. Right, let's see about this one.' It became apparent why she'd confused the dress with hosiery. It was black again, a high-necked, long-sleeved fitted dress that went down almost to her knees, but it was as transparent as dark hose except for two opaque bands, each about six inches wide, one across her breasts and the other around her pubes and bottom.

Kitty switched a standard lamp on. The light was pink, of course. 'Stand in front of this, please?'

Wanda was getting into the spirit of teasing Kitty. It was very flattering, having another young woman drool over her. And it was just girls having a bit of fun, after all. She posed between the lamp and where Kitty stood, facing her with her thighs spread as wide apart as the dress allowed, then with a hollowed back, in silhouette, to show off the svelte lines of her bum, breasts and midriff.

153

Kitty exclaimed, 'I love it! Next one, please?'

Next came an outfit that screamed 'cha-cha' to Wanda. There was a tiny skirt that barely covered her pubes and a very short bolero jacket, both covered with gold and red ruffles. As soon as she'd put it on, Wanda felt moved to hold her arms up, fingers posed to click imaginary castanets, and shake her shoulders and hips. In a mock-Latin accent, she asked, 'You like my looks, Senorita?'

Kitty cried, 'Ole!'

There was another, similar, but with a circular ankle-length skirt that wasn't ruffled and barely covered her pubic mound. Next came a long metallic gold dress that clung, had a neckline that 'V'd down to her waist and had a slit up her left leg that reached her hip. It came with two pairs of matching thong panties. No matter how she danced, it wouldn't expose her sex. A few experimental moves demonstrated that the same couldn't be said for the cheeks of her bum. This was acceptable in Brazil? Weren't the men there known as avid bottom pinchers, or was that Italy?

And there was a 'tap' costume, which came with both a flirty little skirt and a pair of micro-shorts: and then a silver sheath, and a top that was just a skimpy bra and came with a short wrap-over skirt that only just overlapped. She'd have to be very careful what she wore under it.

Two of the dresses were black stretch lace, very

Spanish, very see-through, except in three strategic places. Similarly, another one looked like a spider's web, denser over her nipples and mound, with an oblique ragged 'handkerchief' hemline, from just below her left hip to just lower than her right knee. Given a straw broom and a pumpkin, she could be a very naughty witch, come Halloween. Which she'd be celebrating with Henry! That was a lovely thought. As he loved 'dress up', he had to feel very special about Halloween.

All the time that Wanda was changing in and out of costumes and blatantly flaunting her body, Kitty was fondling herself under the inadequate concealment of her silk shirt. Wanda pretended not to notice but was secretly very pleased. More than pleased – she was turned on by the silent applause. When someone masturbates at the sight of you, that's as sincere as admiration can get.

Dressed in the last outfit, an entirely off-one-shoulder, and half off her left breast, micro-dress in liquid silver with a diagonal hem that was parallel to the neckline, Wanda asked, 'So how is it going with you and Chuck these days, Kitty?'

'Poor Chuck. He's pining for me.'

'He's a good-looking boy. I bet there are lots of girls after him, all eager to console him.'

'The girls he knows aren't going to do for him what I do.'

'Torment him? Tie him up?'

'That's his bag, Wanda. Don't knock it. That lad's a natural born masochistic submissive, like a lot of powerful men are.'

'And you like that?' Wanda asked. 'You enjoy bossing him around?'

Kitty looked at Wanda as if weighing up how best to answer that. 'Me, I'm a switch. You know what that means?'

'Bisexual?'

'That too, but I meant a dom/sub switch. I can be a mistress or a slave, depending on who I'm with, though I'm mainly dominant when it comes to men. That's one reason your suspicions about me and Henry are so silly. Two dominants or two submissives can be friends, good friends even, but never lovers.'

'You've never tried to dominate Henry, in all the years you've known him?'

'Any woman who tried that would have to be crazy and completely insensitive.'

'You mean that my Henry is …?'

'I'm saying nothing about Henry, except that he has a very powerful personality. You already know that.'

'Of course.' Wanda started packing up her outfits. If Kitty really thought that her Henry was one of those dominant types, she'd have said so, wouldn't she? This would have been the ideal time for such a revelation. To Kitty, she said, 'I really don't understand all this kinky stuff, Kitty. You're such a sweetheart. I know about the perverse little games you played with Chuck, who wanted exactly that, but I can't imagine you dominating ordinary people, like me, for instance.'

'I suppose you're right,' Kitty conceded. She paused, then looked directly into Wanda's eyes. 'Wanda, take all this stuff back into the dining room and pack it all back up. Be sure to put every outfit into its original box.'

Wanda felt herself blank out for a moment but she soon recovered and scooped up an armful of dresses. She had five of them neatly folded and restored to their correct wrappings on the dining table before she realised. *She'd been dominated!*

Not knowing how she felt, exactly, she dropped what she was doing and rushed back to Kitty's bedroom. 'You did it! To me!' she accused.

Kitty laughed. 'You needed to know that about yourself, Wanda. Don't worry, I'm not going to dominate you into making love with me.'

'You couldn't, even if you tried.'

'Of course not. Now go finish your job.'

While she folded and packed, Wanda thought hard. Was she safe here, with Kitty? Could her friend really control her that much? Of course not! Wanda had her love for Henry to protect her. And his love for her. *Nothing* could change that.

In any case, she had more power over Kitty than Kitty

did over her. Kitty was so horny for her body she'd do anything to get it. Well, she couldn't have it, but to pay her back for that nasty little trick, some sort of hypnosis, likely, Wanda would make the girl well and truly suffer. She'd just have to be very careful not to cross the line between tempting Kitty mercilessly and giving her what she wanted. 'Lookee, lookee, no touchee.'

Wanda packed the dress she'd been wearing and returned to the bedroom, naked and not just 'unashamed' – but damned proud!

Chapter Seventeen

Kitty was sitting on her bed, propped up on stiff arms extended behind her. That one button on her shirt was undone, now. The pose, with her shoulders pushed forward, suited her slender body and made the most of her delicate little breasts.

She looked up at Wanda and said, 'Now that's the best outfit of them all.'

'I'm glad you like it.'

Kitty grinned. 'After all that exertion, I think we need to shower.'

'*I've* been changing my clothes. What have you been doing?'

'Restraining myself from ravishing you, Wanda.' She shrugged her shirt off. 'Come on, I'll show you my bathroom.'

'You expect us to shower together? No touchee, remember? I can't see us in the shower together without some sort of contact, and that's against the rules.'

'Your rules. Don't worry. Come and see.'

Wanda followed Kitty. Although her friend was slender, there were dimples in the cheeks of her bottom that winked back at her.

The bathroom was spectacular – bigger than Wanda's bedroom by a half. There was a tub that was shaped and coloured like an oyster shell, big enough for four. The matching vanity had to be eight feet long and had three shell-shaped sinks. Then there was the shower. It was free standing, with curved sliding glass doors all the way round, and yes, like the tub, it could accommodate four people at once, easily. Inside. There were four Ionic pillars, close to the glass, with shelves for bottles and jars and hooks for sponges and loofahs.

Kitty pointed and said, 'You go in this side and stand under this showerhead. I'll take the other side and the opposite one. If we keep close to the walls, there'll be three clear feet between us. What do you say?'

Showering like that certainly suited Wanda's plan to tempt Kitty to distraction. It'd also be a very dangerous situation where her own libido was concerned. Well. The whole idea was for her to demonstrate her willpower, or 'won't' power. What the hell! She stepped in and closed the door behind her.

Kitty entered from the opposite side. 'Just push the button. The temperature is preset. There's shampoo and everything on that shelf and on this one, so there's no need for either of us to cross the line.' She pointed the pretty toes of her right foot and drew an imaginary line across the floor with them. 'And never the twain will meet, or need to, not unless we want them to.' She looked at Wanda hopefully.

'Thank you.' Wanda pushed the button. Water, at the absolutely perfect temperature, cascaded over her.

Kitty said, 'If you turn that knob, below the button, the stream will spread or concentrate. Push on the same knob to make it pulsate. I like it hard and in a nice rhythm, like this.' The girl adjusted her shower and unhooked its head, which was on a metallic hose. She passed it across her breasts, which trembled violently at the throbbing pressure, then down her tummy, indenting it. She raised her voice over the noise of the two showers. 'This is the best part. Try it. You'll like it.' She lifted a foot up onto a little built-in ledge and directed the spray up between her thighs. 'Go on, Wanda. You aren't afraid to, are you? So what if you have an orgasm? I've seen you climax before. You look so sexy when you're right on the edge. I'll control myself, honest.'

Just to show how self-controlled she was, Wanda said, 'That sounds like fun but I think I'll get clean first. You go ahead without me, if you like.'

'Tough, huh? OK, if you can wait for it, so can I.' Kitty stretched to reach the shampoo, which wasn't that high that she really need to stretch up for it. Nor did she have to do it sideways on, showing off the elongation of her torso.

Wanda had no doubt that her friend was posing as seductively as she could. Well, two could play at that game! Facing Kitty, she shampooed her own hair vigorously, both elbows held high, getting the maximum jiggle. Then she had to rinse not only her hair, but also her breasts, and chase the soapy bubbles all the way down her body with the stream of water. Elbows up again, for conditioning, and she managed to 'accidentally' drop the bottle. She turned around, so she was facing three-quarters away, and stooped over without bending her legs to retrieve the lotion, not forgetting to flex the muscles in her bottom cheeks as she did so.

'Nice!' Kitty complimented. 'You're quite limber, aren't you?'

'My mom took me to yoga from quite young.'

'So you can get into all sorts of fancy positions, then. I'm sure that Henry will love your "Downward Dog".'

'And my "Little Thunderbolt" and "Wheel".'

'I'm not familiar with those,' Kitty confessed. 'Will you show them to me?'

'Some day, maybe.'

'Nude?'

Wanda ignored that one and started soaping herself. Kitty followed suit, making the process one of fondling herself more than cleansing. She squeezed lather up her cute little tits, from their bases to their tips, then flicked the bubbles off her erect nipples.

'Ouch!'

'You hurt yourself?' Wanda asked.

'In the best possible way, darling. Now where's that loofah? This one is very rough, ideal for exfoliating. It leaves my skin extra sensitive.' Kitty took the phallic cleaning instrument from its hook and soaped it thoroughly, making quite the performance out of stroking it as if she was stroking a man's cock.

'Trying to make it grow longer?' Wanda asked, in her best innocent voice.

Kitty laughed dutifully. She scrubbed her chest with the coarse side, turning her breasts bright pink and engorging her nipples until they were deep scarlet. 'That's nice,' she said. 'This is nicer.' She turned around and passed the cylinder between her thighs so that she could hold one end at her belly and the other at her bum, and sawed it backwards and forwards.

That *did* look like it'd feel nice, so Wanda followed suit. It was a rough caress, but a very stimulating one. Before long, her pussy was tingling and her clit engorging. The texture was too rough on her button, but it was easy enough to change the angle so that there was no direct contact.

Kitty, by contrast, seemed to like it rough. She turned to face Wanda, leaned back against the glass, spread her thighs wide and pushed her pubes forward. It was a most inelegant pose but despite that – perhaps because of that – it looked sexy as hell. A sweet and sophisticated young lady was transformed into an animal in heat. Wanda liked that.

Kitty grunted, 'I'm going to come, Wanda. Join me?'

'Let's see if I can catch up.' Wanda bunched her loofah around one fist to grind it into her sex, parting its lips and scouring their insides. She took the shower head, on hard pulsate, and aimed it directly onto her clit. The powerful sensations, plus the sight of her animalistic lust-consumed friend, heated her up deep inside. The tingling started and began to focus. 'I'm getting there,' she screamed.

'Me too. Soon!'

'Yeah, soon for me, as well.'

'I love you, Wanda,' Kitty said. She took a deep breath. 'Well, lust you, anyway. Lust like a lover and love like a sister.'

'That's OK. Me too! You! Lust!'

'Oh fuck!' burst from Kitty's lips.

'Yeah, fuck, fuck, fuck!' Wanda added, 'I want a cock to suck on!' Something nasty from deep inside Wanda was desperate for her to be as obscene as possible.

'Can't help you there. Clit do?'

Wanda shook her head, denying the image that invaded her mind.

'I want a cock, too,' Kitty shouted. 'A big hard one! I should have brought a dildo in here. Or one each. No matter. I'm getting near the edge, Wanda. You know what I mean?'

'Yes, of course I do. Wait for me, Kitty-bitch. Let's go together.'

'Sorry, I'm losing it, now … Now. Now!' Kitty convulsed, thrusting her belly at Wanda and humping the air.

It was the depravity of the sight, more than the sensations she was inflicting on herself, that took Wanda over the edge. She slumped, just like her dearest lovely darling friend was slumped. Seated on the bottom of the shower, their toes touched, and Wanda simply didn't care if it *was* against her rules. She just sat there, panting and playing footsie.

Chapter Eighteen

What they'd done in front of each other in the shower felt a bit embarrassing once their lust had been discharged. Kitty found them two short towelling robes, which they belted tightly and securely. When they sat on the couch, they sat at each end, as far apart as they could, and tucked their robes under their thighs. They didn't look directly at each other.

'What do we do now?' Wanda asked.

'Hungry yet?'

'Peckish,' Wanda admitted.

'Chinese?'

'Sounds good to me.' Eating is a safe, non-sexual activity. She could eat without stealing secret glances at Kitty's lovely long legs. It'd be a distraction from the erotically charged atmosphere. And, despite the power of her recent orgasm, horniness was slowly creeping back into her. Was she insatiable? Would Henry be able to cope with that, if she was? After all, a jug can only be emptied once before it needs time to refill. No man can match a libidinous and healthy woman, not orgasm for orgasm. Was that going to be a problem?

Kitty fished a complicated remote control out from under a cushion. A nude portrait, which *could* have been Kitty but the model was wearing a big hat with a veil so that Wanda wasn't sure, slid aside to expose a large flat screen. It chimed on and showed a menu of Chinese food, with pictures.

'What's "*moo goo gai cow*"?' Wanda asked.

'Not what it sounds like, I don't expect. It can't be beef cooked in milk, can it?'

'I doubt it.'

'Let's order some and find out.' She paused and glanced sideways at Wanda. 'We OK? You and me?'

Wanda reached out and touched her friend's elbow, briefly. 'Of course we are. We're grown women, after all.'

'And sophisticated ones.'

'Exactly.'

'Hug?'

'Of course.'

They shimmied closer and cuddled each other, but gingerly, still a little unsure.

Kitty ordered the special fried rice and the Szechwan beef with broccoli. Wanda added prawn crackers and bang-bang chicken, just because of its name. Then they had to have at least one sweet and sour dish, and a curry and a chili plus spring rolls. And no meal is complete without dessert, so they added apple fritters with 'moon-light' syrup and whipped cream.

'That should feed about six of us,' Kitty observed.

'Should we cancel a couple of dishes?'

'If we did, what would we eat for breakfast?'

Oh yes, breakfast, which reminded Wanda that she'd be there overnight. 'Consuela would have a fit,' she said.

'When in Rome! At the ranch, we eat Consuela style. In my apartment, we eat Kitty style.'

A smart remark about eating Kitty and pussy-eating sprang into Wanda's mind, but she shut it off before it could escape her lips.

Kitty turned the menu into a TV and searched. She found two programmes scheduled about dancing, one with celebrities and the other with wannabe professionals in competition. They didn't clash, for a change. 'You're going to take Latin dancing classes, right? Want to watch some to prime you?'

'Mainly, I want to see what they wear to dance in. You don't get any Brazilian stations, do you?'

'Sorry. The watered-down US ones will have to do. We could always watch a porno channel instead?' Her sidelong glance was packed with meaning.

'Not right now. Not while we eat.'

'Chinese,' Kitty added, getting some of her 'naughty' back.

That made Wanda feel better. She hated to have tension

of the wrong sort between her and her new 'best friend forever'. Her first 'bff'? Her first since high school, anyway, not counting the boys or men she'd dated. Come to that, none of those had been 'friends'. But Henry was, she thought, in a strange way. He was her friend and her … mentor? Something like that, anyway, plus protector and provider. Her *everything*?

'I'll split the price of the meal with you,' she offered Kitty.

'Silly! I have an account with the restaurant. I'm not going to sort out what I ate with who, am I?'

'I guess not.' That was what being rich had to be like. Trivial sums like a hundred or so dollars, or whatever the meal came to, meant nothing. She'd have to learn to adjust to that. The idea that money was virtually meaningless would be hard to adapt to, but she'd try very hard. Henry would help her.

Kitty put a sitcom on and snuggled closer, close enough that Wanda could smell the jasmine in her hair. On impulse, Wanda planted a kiss on the top of Kitty's head.

'Thanks.'

'Welcome.'

Kitty's cheek was resting on Wanda's shoulder, but in a sisterly way. Definitely sisterly, though her sweet breath was wafting into Wanda's cleavage. She could ignore that.

The phone rang. Kitty answered. After a few seconds, she put her hand over the mouthpiece and said, 'It's your mom. She wants to know if you're here.'

Wanda almost said, 'Tell her no,' but bit it back. She reached for the phone.

Kitty said, 'Excuse me a minute,' and left the room.

Wanda said, 'Yes, Mom?'

'Having a good time with Kitty?'

'Yes, thanks. We just ordered Chinese.'

'What have you two girls been up to?'

Honesty was very tempting, but, once more, Wanda resisted. She said, 'Kitty has been teaching me how to comport myself as a rich woman.'

'That's nice. Learn much?'

'Lots, thanks.'

'I've been teaching you that all your life.'

'Yes, Mom, but Kitty's been living it, all hers.'

'Even so. Are there any men there?'

'No, Mom, just us two girls. There's the doorbell,' Wanda lied.

'Let Kitty get it.'

'She's changing for supper.'

'Oh, I see.'

'Bye, Mom.' Wanda hung up. Cancelling her white lie, the doorbell *did* chime. She called, 'Kitty!'

'You get it, there's a dear.'

Wanda scooped up her purse and opened the door. A young lad had four big bags in an insulated carrier. He looked her up and down while Wanda hastily fished for change. His admiration for her legs was a little too obvious for her comfort. Still, it wasn't his fault that her robe was so short. You show 'em, you have to expect to have them looked at.

'No tip, thanks, Miss,' he said. 'It's taken care of. We just add twenty per cent to the lady's bill.'

'Thank you. Bye!'

She spread the packages across the table. Kitty returned, fully made up and wearing an abbreviated kimono in red and black satin.

'You and Henry and your dressing up!' Wanda commented.

'You too. Don't tell me you didn't like parading around in that gorgeous green riding habit of yours.'

'I confess. Yes, I like it. It's fun and Henry likes it.'

'Two excellent reasons. Let's eat.' She poured two glasses of Tokay. 'This is just to go with the food. I've got a pitcher of martinis in the freezer, for later.'

'In the freezer?'

'It won't freeze because of the gin and I like my martinis bitter cold. You?'

'I'll tell you later, after I've tried one. All of a sudden, I'm famished.'

Kitty produced chopsticks and they dug in. With about a quarter of their order consumed, both were full. 'Leftovers for breakfast, and lunch, at least,' Kitty said. 'I hate to cook.'

The girls settled down to watch TV, pick at leftovers

and sip icy martinis. Not all of the dancing was Latin but the costumes the dancers wore were an eye-opener for Wanda. Most of them were tight, or skimpy, or both. There were deep cleavages on both men and women but the women had the exclusive on 'backless'. Some of the outfits were scooped so low that hints of rear cleavage showed. Wanda loved the bare midriffs that a lot of costumes displayed, and the rippling abdomens. It'd been at least a year since she'd done crunches each morning. She'd better start again, even if her mom did think that six-packs were unfeminine. Many of the Latin dances were incredibly *tense*. Wanda loved that, body straining against body. That was a good sign for their marriage. Henry'd said he liked Latin dancing. Anyone who did was obviously very sexual.

By the end of the second programme, she was feeling as warm as she would have if they'd watched porn.

Kitty said, 'I've only one bed, Wanda, but I'll lend you some pyjamas or a nightie, if you prefer, and we can sleep on opposite sides of the bed. It's king-sized, so there's lots of room. We won't have to touch – unless you want to?'

'Thanks, thanks and no thanks.'

'Got it. You know what?'

'What?'

'I'm feeling a bit – you know. How about you? Maybe it'd be a good idea if we took the edge off a bit before we go to bed.'

'What do you mean?'

'You know very well what I mean,' Kitty said. '"Lookee, no touchee?" We could watch each other play "pet the pussy" again. If we climaxed just before going to bed, we'd sleep better. I've got some vibrators in the bedroom. You'd get first choice?'

Wanda pretended to think but the idea was very appealing and didn't need thinking about. Kitty was so *hot* when she masturbated. She was a joy to watch!

She said, 'Show me your toys. Let's see if any tempt me.'

'You'll find this educational, I think,' Kitty said. She led the way back into her bedroom. They sat side by side on a cushioned bench seat. The top drawer of a chest was lined with velvet and displayed a selection of vibrators and dildos, each one in a plastic bag and laid out in a neat row. 'I sterilise them after each use,' Kitty told Wanda. 'They're very hygienic.'

'That's nice to know.' Wanda picked one up from the end. It was no larger than a lipstick.

'For travelling,' Kitty said. 'Trains and planes.'

Next was a butterfly. Kitty explained that it was a vibrator that a girl wore and was controlled by a remote, which she might give to her date to tease her with.

'That doesn't sound like you,' Wanda commented.

'Oh, I'm always the one with the remote. Great fun!' She looked thoughtful. 'You know, with the butterfly, there's no actual *touching*.'

'Close enough, though.' Wanda picked up an oversized cylinder that was filled with tiny multi-coloured beads.

'That one's interesting,' Kitty said. 'But it doesn't have a clit-stimulator, like this one.' She held up an oversized vibrator with a projecting prong. 'Or the rabbit is similar? 'This one is just for the G spot. I use it together with a more slender internal toy, sometimes. And I've got anal vibes, and butt plugs and probes, and …'

'I'll take the Hitachi Wand, if that's OK.'

Kitty's eyes narrowed. 'Ten days ago, I was teaching you what a vibrator is and showing you how to use one. Now you know them by name? Either you've been studying hard, or …'

'You were having so much fun "teaching" me, I couldn't spoil it by letting on that I have a few toys of my own. It was funny, though, you thinking that a healthy young woman of my age could be so ignorant.'

'You bitch!'

'We're a pair of bitches, right?'

Kitty shrugged. 'Well, thanks anyway. It *was* fun, being your teacher. Any more surprises for me? A dozen lesbian lovers in your past? You have season tickets to the local orgies?'

'I've had a couple of men in my life and I experimented a bit once, with another girl, nothing much, just kissing and fondling, mainly. That's it for me, honest and true. My life has been relatively sheltered, till now.'

'Because of your mom, not because of your natural inclination?'

'Yes, I suppose so,' Wanda confessed.

'She has a lot to answer for,' Kitty observed.

'My mom has always done what she thought was best for me,' Wanda defended. 'Anyway, I think she's loosening up a bit now, since she's known Lucinda.'

'Ah yes, Lucinda. I hope I'm as horny and able to perform as she is when I reach her age.'

'How old is she?' Wanda asked.

'No one knows. If Henry does, he isn't telling. You certainly can't tell by looking at her. A combination of silicon, Botox and booze has her frozen in time. After the Apocalypse, future archaeologists are going to dig her up and wonder if she was typical of our era. She'll end up in the future equivalent of the Louvre.'

'Perhaps she's a vampire,' Wanda suggested.

'That's what she dresses as, come Halloween. And a damned sexy vamp she makes, too.' Kitty ripped the plastic cover off the Wand and handed it to Wanda. 'Let's get this show on the road. There's lube in the bedside-table drawer. I have the kind that tingles. Have you tried it?'

'No.'

'Do. It's nice, not as spectacular as in the ads, but it still does some pleasant things to your clit.' Kitty stood up and shed her kimono.

Wanda followed suit. After their revealing conversation,

175

and a few martinis, she no longer felt the least bit uncomfortable about being naked with Kitty. She still enjoyed looking at her friend's body, though. It hadn't grown stale for her.

And her skin would be *so* nice to touch ...

They sat side by side, their hips a good foot apart, on the edge of Kitty's bed. Kitty nodded towards the mirror doors of her closet. 'Nice-looking pair, huh?'

'Yours or mine.'

'Us, silly. Here's the lube.'

Wanda took it and squeezed a drop out onto the pad of her right index finger.

'Don't scrimp,' Kitty told her.

'I won't. This is for a precise spot.' She spread her thighs. The fingers of her left hand drew back on the sheath of her clit, popping the tiny pink pearl out into the open.

'Nice clit!' Kitty said. 'That lube, it's strawberry flavour.'

Wanda licked her finger and nodded. 'Artificial, of course.'

'Can I have a taste?'

Wanda extended her arm sideways.

'That's not what I meant, and you know it.'

'Sorry, Kitty-cat.' Wanda dabbed more lube onto her nipples and picked up the Wand. 'A Wand for Wanda,' she said.

'Funny.' Kitty squirted lube up inside her pussy and smoothed it around with two fingers. 'Brrr. Tingles!'

'I think I'll take some of this on my honeymoon,' Wanda said.

'It's good for anal, as well.'

'Do you think my Henry will want to bugger me?'

'Do you want him to?'

Wanda nodded, not quite ready to put her desire into words.

'Then, if he doesn't introduce it by the third night, ask him to. *That'd* turn him on, for sure.'

'He wouldn't think less of me?'

'Every man I've asked to do me up my bum has been both delighted and excited.'

'How many is that?'

Kitty thought for a moment. 'Two,' she said.

'That's not many.'

'The rest took the initiative.'

'Oh.' The big ball at the end of the Wand buzzed on the tip of Wanda's left nipple. She was only using a delicate touch but she still felt little shocks of yearning zip down to her clit. Her eyes half-closed and she leaned back on one arm but she could still watch Kitty, and herself, in the mirror. Her friend had pinched the lips of her sex together and was running the balls of her vibrator up and down the crease. The toy she'd chosen looked like a stack of ping-pong balls separated by plastic half-inch necks but it was all one piece.

'You ever put that one up your bum?' Wanda asked.

'Mm. It's very good that way. My knot opens and closes for each little ball, so ... Why tell you when I can show you?' Kitty slathered the plastic with lube, turned around and knelt up on the bed, facing away from the mirror, her face on the bedspread, bum high. 'Can you see my reflection OK?' she asked.

Wanda said, 'Yes,' but she'd turned sideways to watch Kitty's play directly.

The girl reached back between her own thighs with her toy buzzing in her fist. She introduced the top ball to the ring of her bum-hole. 'Watch it go in, Wanda,' she purred.

Wanda watched, fascinated. This was a process she'd never observed before. As she watched, she folded a lip of her pussy over her delicate clit and pressed on it with the head of the Wand.

The plastic ball indented Kitty's bottom, pushing and being resisted, until, with an almost audible 'plop', the ball disappeared. Kitty said, 'That's one.'

'There's six in all,' Wanda said. 'How many can you manage?'

'Watch, and wonder, Wanda.'

'Oh, I will.'

The second ball was pressing, harder, and it too plopped through the tight restriction. It was fascinating. What would it feel like? Wanda could imagine but reality beats imagination when it comes to sex.

That was an interesting thought.

To Wanda's surprise and disappointment, Kitty tugged. The second ball from the top distended her rectum, pulled it up into a little pink striated mound, then popped out.

'Is that it?' Wanda demanded.

'Of course not. Just playing.'

'Oh!'

'I don't rush it.'

'Take your time,' Wanda told her, and eased up the vibrating pressure on her clit. It wouldn't do to come too soon.

The second ball was forced back in, then the third went in, came out, went back in again. Kitty, her voice muffled by her bedclothes, said, 'I had a man once who I trained to just push the head of his cock into my bum, then pull it out, over and over, until I told him he could go ahead and just do me. That was fun.'

'I bet.'

The fourth ball disappeared. And the fifth. The end had to be very deep inside Kitty by then.

'Is that thing flexible?' Wanda asked.

'No, it's stiff. Good job my rectum is bendable.' The sixth ball went in.

Wanda gasped, 'Fuck! Sorry. Is that good?'

'Lovely. Now all I need is …'

Kitty's other hand appeared between her legs, holding a two-pronged toy with a small ball at the top of each prong. 'For bum and pussy; G spot and clit.' She inserted one prong into her pussy and manoeuvred the other until it pressed against her clit, which was *really* engorged. Damn, it had turned dark scarlet. Kitty had to be having a hell of a good time. Wanda worked the Wand's ball harder against where her clit was partially protected. A drop more lube would have been nice but she didn't want to stop to apply it.

Kitty was panting into her bedspread. Both of her hands were working the toys she held, six vibrating balls inside her bum, one on her G spot and the other on her clit. All she really needed was someone to pinch and roll her nipples, Wanda thought, and she'd be complete. It was a tempting thought but she managed to just imagine that she was doing it to her friend instead of breaking her own rule.

Too late, anyway. Kitty was quivering into a climax. Wanda pressed her toy down a little harder with one hand while she twisted her right nipple with the fingers of the other and joined her friend in a gentle paroxysm of pleasure. Gentle, but very, very, pleasant.

Kitty found pink satin pyjamas for each of them and they went to bed, temporarily sated.

Chapter Nineteen

Wanda dreamt.

All she had on was an abbreviated transparent pink T-shirt. She just had to hope that if she met anyone they wouldn't notice that she was naked from her waist down. Wanda was still in Kitty's apartment but it had changed by growing enormous. Every room was two floors high and big enough to hold a ball in. There were dozens of those vast chambers, maybe hundreds. Every one of them held tables that were loaded down with gift-wrapped boxes, all addressed to Wanda. She wandered from room to room, touching and shaking but not opening. For some reason, she was nervous about what they might contain.

Finally, she summoned up her courage and tore the paper and lid off one. It held a Russian nesting doll that had been painted to look like a nun, complete with wimple and habit. When she screwed the head off the nun, there was a Betty Boop inside, looking as saucy and playfully sexy as ever. Inside Betty, there was a Jessica Rabbit, but with Wanda's face and hair. Wanda shook Jessica. She rattled, so there was at least one more doll to discover but the thought of what kind of doll it might be made Wanda nervous. She set the dolls aside.

The next parcel revealed a Faberge egg. When she picked it up, it vibrated. She pressed it to her pubes and felt tiny, very pleasant electric shocks that curled her toes. Should she keep it there and get off on it? It seemed like some sort of desecration, to use a priceless work of art to masturbate with, but she was rich and special now, wasn't she? Fabulously wealthy people did that sort of thing. They were entitled.

Before she could decide, Kitty arrived. She was leading a man in a grey three-piece suit by the hand. He needed leading because he was blindfolded.

Kitty said, 'I found this outside, Wanda. I thought you might like it, to play with. He doesn't know who we are or where he is, so you can do pretty much what you like with him.'

'You're so kind, Kitty.'

'You know I love you, darling. Shall I peel him for you?'

'Please do.'

The man's clothes had to have been made for a male stripper because all the seams were Velcro. With one strong rip, Kitty had him naked. How that worked with his shoes and socks, Wanda didn't know, but it wasn't important. He stood there, bare and fidgeting, with an impressive but limp cock dangling down in front of his muscular thighs.

Kitty said, 'That will never do!' She gave his shaft a few quick strokes. It rose and lengthened impressively. 'How do you want him?' she asked Wanda.

Wanda pushed a pile of presents aside and hitched herself onto the space she'd made. She pointed at the floor. 'Kneel him here,' she said.

Kitty led him and pushed him down. Wanda took him by his ears and guided his mouth to her sex.

'Get to work,' Kitty ordered.

He did, hands behind his back, nuzzling into her, he lapped and sucked and lapped some more, engorging her clit more than it had ever engorged before, until it projected from her folds for a full half-inch.

'Suck on it!' Kitty ordered.

He did, fellating Wanda's clit as if it was a tiny cock. Kitty watched and fondled herself idly. Wanda relaxed back until she was lying on the table with her legs dangling from her hips down.

'Fuck now!' she said.

'You heard the lady.' Kitty pulled the man to his feet by his hair. 'Excuse me,' she said as she took hold of his cock and introduced it to Wanda's pussy. 'Now do it.'

He thrust. Wanda braced herself. He had to have a weird cock because it vibrated up inside her. Maybe he had an implant. That seemed like a good idea – prosthetic vibrating cocks, for men.

'Do you want him to come inside you?' Kitty asked.

'Not particularly. Once I've climaxed, I don't care where he comes.'

'Then it's OK if I take it?'

'Be my guest.'

'You're so sweet, Wanda. Henry is a very lucky man.'

It didn't happen very often in her dreams, and Wanda had realised she was dreaming by then, but she climaxed. 'All yours,' she told Kitty.

Kitty squatted quickly and yanked the anonymous man around so that his semen sprayed all over her tiny breasts. 'Thanks, Wanda,' she said. As she led the man away, they both shrank down to the size of ants, and disappeared.

Wanda said, 'You're welcome,' and woke up.

Kitty was spooning her and holding her breast in her hand, but she was asleep, so it wasn't a betrayal. Wanda was damp and warm between her thighs. She slipped out of bed to avoid complications and went to heat up Chinese leftovers for their breakfast. At least it wasn't a cold pizza.

Chapter Twenty

Madame Lupe, Wanda's dancing teacher, said, 'The tango, she is a dance of love and courtship. The man, he tries to dominate the woman. She pretends to resist as she lures him into her clutches, when she "surrenders" and he is hers. The lambada, she is different. This is the dance of pure lust. The man and the woman are equals, both ver' hot for each other. We dance from *here*.' She clutched the crotch of her emerald-green Velour pants. 'It is the love making while standing up, including the frottage. When the last notes of the music fade away, there is no doubt what comes next. They will fall to the floor and ravage each other in the frenzy of the fuck. You understand, huh?'

'Yes I do, thanks, Madame Lupe.'

'You are coming along ver' good. Your lovers will be proud of you. Next time, I want to see you in four-inch heels, not those silly baby shoes, OK?'

'I'll try.'

Wanda rushed through her shower and changing. She

had a lunch date with the moms and Henry, at a Thai restaurant that was on the other side of the city. After that, they had an appointment to try out flavours of wedding cake, then on to finalise the menu for the reception.

There was no reasonable way to do it by public transport. She was forced to drive. Inevitably, despite her GPS, Wanda got lost and was late. The moms were eating ice cream and drinking coffee. There was a blank place where Henry must have been sitting.

'About time,' her mom snorted.

'Sorry. Where's Henry?'

Lucinda said, 'We needed the guest list so Henry went to fetch it.'

Wanda's mom added, 'I gave him a key to our place and the password for your laptop. He's clever. He'll know how to print it out.'

Wanda sank into a chair. Oh? Henry. Her laptop. The files for Dr Sullivan, full of her dreams and fantasies and the actual truth about what she and Kitty had done together? Cold slimy panic gripped her guts.

'Oh! Hm, Mom, I changed my password a while back,' she lied, though she'd meant to. 'I'd better go help him.'

She tore out of the restaurant, ignoring her mom's cry of: 'You could phone it to him.' She gunned her engine. How long did she have to save her life from total disaster? Could she cross the city in six minutes or less? She could but try.

Impending doom focused her attention on the route

but it still took the best part of an hour. Wanda parked. Should she just run away and never return? Could she fake an illness and then a coma? What she *had* to do, of course, was go in and face the consequences of her libidinous and perverted imagination. There would be a price to pay. Henry would dump her. Her mom would disown her. Perhaps she'd still have a friend in Kitty, but she'd be poor. Filthy rich people don't chum around with paupers.

Suicide seemed like it might be an excellent solution, if there was a way to do it that wouldn't hurt.

What the fuck! Wanda braced herself and went in. She called, 'Henry? Are you here, darling? Where are you?' Could he have got himself lost? That didn't seem likely. Henry wasn't the type. She slowly trudged through the living room to her bedroom. Oh, God! He was there, intently reading something on her screen. It wasn't the guest list. She froze.

In a dangerously calm voice, he said, 'Good afternoon, Wanda.'

She gabbled, 'That's not real, none of it. It's dreams and stuff. None of it ever happened. You can ask my shrink, Dr Sullivan. He'll tell you. I have a condition. I can't help those thoughts. It's not my fault, really it isn't. It's like Tourette's.' She dried up and waited.

He looked at her and said, 'You realise that this changes everything, don't you, Wanda?'

Her last hope died. 'I –'

'I was going to wait until after we were married,' he continued.

What on earth did he mean by that? Wait for what?

'I've known all along that you'd need training, Wanda. I've been impatient to start, so I'm not that disappointed to have to commence now.'

'Training? What do you mean?'

'Discipline. I've seen your potential all along. After a short period of instruction, you will make me the ideal wife. You're beautiful and have an incredibly powerful sex drive. It certainly helps that you are also sweet and charming.'

Hope bloomed, along with total confusion. 'Thank you, Henry, but I still don't understand what it is that you're talking about.'

'You soon will. Our mothers are going to keep those appointments without us. They'll phone before returning. Those are the instructions I gave them.'

'You tell your mother what to do?'

'My father trained her well. Now, you still have that riding crop I gave you?'

'Of course.'

'Here?'

'Yes.'

'Good. Go fetch it.'

Wanda turned and walked away like an automaton.

He wanted the crop? She couldn't think what for. Come to that, she couldn't think at all. Her mind was a total blank. It was as if her brain had frozen solid. She could do as she was told. That was the extent of her volition. The crop was on the top shelf of the hall closet. She took it down and carried it on two open palms back to where Henry waited. He'd taken his jacket off and rolled up his sleeves. What muscular forearms he had!

'Take your skirt off,' he said.

She did as she was told, still not understanding what was happening.

'And the panties.'

That sounded nice. He was telling her to take her panties off. That had to mean that something sexual was going to happen. A corner of her brain woke up.

'Bend over my knees,' he said.

The corner of her brain closed down again but she did as she was bidden. His hand pushed her top a little higher and then caressed the cheeks of her bottom. She enjoyed that. He liked her bum. That was a good thing.

'Do you know what I'm about to do, Wanda?'

She shook her head and then managed to squeak out, 'No, Henry.'

'I thought not. I was absolutely right about you, my darling.'

'Of course you were, Henry.'

'Ready?'

She nodded without understanding. His arm rose. There was a swish and a line of fire bloomed across her upper thighs.

'Is this real life, Henry? Not a dream? Not a fantasy?'

'This is absolutely real, Wanda.' The crop came down again.

Wanda's new life, her perfect life, had finally started. She'd never need to fantasise again.

Henry Chandler's Cream of Carrot Soup.

Two pounds of baby carrots, chopped.
Two pounds of Vidalia onions, chopped.
A quarter pound of butter.
2% milk.
½ and ½ cream.
Salt and pepper.
One teaspoon of dried oregano.
Dry sherry or Worcester sauce.

Melt the butter in a large heavy saucepan. Add the onions and stir as you simmer until the onions are transparent.
Add the carrots.
Add 2% milk. Enough to just cover the vegetables.
Keep simmering until the carrots turn to mush, adding milk as necessary.
Add salt and pepper to taste, plus the oregano.

Keep stirring and simmering, adding ½ and ½ cream until you have a thick creamy consistence. If the mix gets too watery, slowly heat it till it thickens.

Pour into soup bowls.

Decorate each bowl of soup with a swirl of either sherry or Worcester in the centre.

Serve.

Leftovers can be frozen and reheated.

Alternatives.

Use chicken stock instead of milk.

Decorate with blobs of thick sour cream instead of the sherry or Worcester.

Substitute small tender parsnips for some or all of the carrots.